# Praise for the Nick Madrid S[...]

" ... Peter Guttridge is off to a rousing s[...]
mystery ge[...]
—*Chicago T*[...]

"Original and highly readable ... but a word of warning: never let this man house-sit if you value your pets."
—Lynne Truss, author of *Eats, Shoots & Leaves*

"Peter Guttridge has ... the kind of mordant wit and cold-eyed social observation to make his Nick Madrid mysteries de rigueur reading."
—*Good Book Guide*

"[The] Nick Madrid mysteries are nothing if not addictively, insanely entertaining"
—*Ruminator*

"... a near laugh-riot."
—*Library Journal*

"Few British crime writers can match the outrageousness of their American counterparts but Peter Guttridge is well on his way ... the satire is spot on."
—*The Guardian*

"Wacky ... Hilarious ... A great read."
—Minette Walters, author of *The Sculptress* and *Fox Evil*

"Brilliant ... Peter Guttridge is a fresh, stimulating new talent."
—Peter James, author of *Faith*, *Host,* and *Possession*

"Guttridge's series is among the funniest and sharpest in the genre, with a level of intelligence often lacking in better-known fare."
—*Balitmore Sun*

"Brilliant one-liners, lightning action, lots of suspense and very funny— self-deprecating Madrid is fast becoming my favorite crime hero."
—*Good Housekeeping*

## Other Nick Madrid Mysteries
Now Available or Coming Soon

# TWO TO TANGO

## PETER GUTTRIDGE

**speck press**
denver

First published in the United States by *speck press* 2005
Printed and bound in Canada
Book layout and design by *CPG*, corvuspublishinggroup.com
ISBN: 1-933108-00-2, ISBN13: 978-1-933108-00-1

This book is a work of fiction. Names, characters, places, and incidents are either
the product of the author's imagination or are used fictitiously. Any resemblance
to actual events or locales or persons, living or dead, is entirely coincidental.
Although the author and publisher have made every effort to ensure the
accuracy and completeness of information contained in this book, we assume no
responsibility for errors, inaccuracies, omissions, or any inconsistency herein. Any
slights of people, places, or organizations are unintentional.

Published in Great Britain by Headline Book Publishing 1998
Copyright © 1998 Peter Guttridge

Library of Congress Cataloging-in-Publication Data
Guttridge, Peter.
Two to tango / by Peter Guttridge.-- 2nd ed.
p. cm.
Includes bibliographical references and index.
ISBN 1-933108-00-2 (alk. paper)
1. Journalists--Fiction. 2. Rock musicians--Crimes against--Fiction. 3. Drug
traffic--Fiction. 4. South America--Fiction. I. Title.

PR6107.U88T88 2005
823'.92--dc22

2005000236

10 9 8 7 6 5 4 3 2 1

For Alan and Jude,
without whom South America would have been a
very different experience.

# ONE

He wore mud-splattered workman's trousers and a hostile expression. I wore Armani and a cheesy grin. He probably wondered what this guy was doing dressed up to the nines balanced on a slippery, rickety plank above a foul-smelling latrine on the banks of the Amazon.

I might have been wondering the same but my mind was on other things. Specifically on the long knife in his extended right hand. My smile faded. Three hours in the Amazon and already the trip was a disaster.

Things had started to go wrong the minute the plane landed at Leticia, where Colombia dips its toe in the piranha-infested waters of the Amazon. Two hundred kilos of cocaine had just been found at the airport in a consignment of fish bound for Bogota. Had my friend Bridget and I been proper journalists, we might have felt obliged to investigate. Since we were having a holiday together—no, not like that, we're just chums—we were simply obliged to stay in our plane with the other passengers, the air conditioning turned off, whilst the authorities investigated the slip-up.

The slip-up being that some customs officer had been stupid enough to find the cocaine. Everybody knew that large volumes of it were shipped out of Leticia every day from cooking factories in the jungle. The authorities were bribed more than enough to look the other way. Whoever had found the shipment clearly wasn't with the program.

Bad luck for him. The zealot would be demoted by the end of the day, dead by the end of the week.

"It's nothing to do with me," I said indignantly when I saw Bridget looking at me.

"It was your idea to come here," she said, wafting the airline magazine in front of her face in a vain attempt to shift the sluggish air.

"My idea for *me* to come here. Your idea to tag along."

She flared her nostrils.

"I don't *tag*."

"I still don't understand why you didn't visit your friend in Cartagena as planned."

"I changed my mind, okay?" She gave me a steely look. "You have a problem with that?"

"Absolutely not," I said quickly, sinking lower into my seat.

When we finally got out of the plane, the humidity in the air on the tarmac wasn't noticeably less. I was perspiring heavily by the time we reached the baggage hall. I could feel the sweat soaking into the collar of my jacket. Damp patches blossomed under my arms.

A squat, chubby man wearing a baseball cap was holding up a piece of cardboard on which our names—Nick Madrid and Bridget Frost—were crudely scrawled. His trousers were at half-mast and he wore a creased blue shirt, tight over his bulging belly.

We signalled him over. Introductions were brief. His name was Joel, our guide for our trip on the Amazon. Bridget looked at the itinerary clutched in her hand.

"Let's get to the hotel and those 'Welcome Cocktails,' Joel," she said briskly.

"No hurry, Mrs. Bridget," Joel said, looking askance at her pile of luggage. "Hotel three hours upriver."

"What?" Bridget said, looking down at the itinerary again.

"Boat leaves in one hour."

"We've got to go on a boat?"

"Bridget, we're on the Amazon for God's sake," I said. "How else do you think we're going to get around?"

It sounded romantic to me. I imagined either a power boat to whisk us to our hotel or maybe one of those old paddle steamers, like in the Herzog film, *Fitzcarraldo*. Perhaps I could buy a panama hat to go with my rather stylish linen suit. I considered a fly whisk but I wasn't sure if I was on the right continent for that.

"Take us to the nearest bar then," Bridget said before stomping off, head high. Joel and I looked down at her luggage. He half-heartedly took hold of the handle of her largest case. Given that it was almost as tall as he was, I took it from him and staggered off after Bridget.

We left the luggage at Joel's travel agency and went to buy my panama in a shop along the street. Then Joel suggested we have our drink in a bar on the waterfront in Peru. The border with Peru is a five-minute bus ride west of Leticia. The port almost merges to the east with neighboring Marco in Brazil.

The bus—actually a battered old transit van with two lumpy bench seats—took us from the clean, modern, single storey buildings of the Colombian town to a rundown waterfront. Joel led us on foot along a dusty street into a shanty town of food stalls and open-walled bars with tin roofs. Hard eyes watched impassively as we went by.

We stepped carefully on rough gangplanks across the muddy shallows of the river to reach a bar on stilts. We plopped down at a table overlooking sluggish brown water.

Joel and I were both soaked with sweat. Bridget restricted

herself, by force of will alone I'm sure, to a wet sheen and a couple of beads of sweat glistening in her cleavage. Joel couldn't take his eyes off her breasts. He pretended to look away but his eyes kept sliding back. She was quite a sight. She was wearing a short, red, low-cut dress that left little to the imagination. I had been hoping to present myself as a man of the world, but with sweat dripping off my ears I looked your average red-faced Englishman abroad.

Here the Amazon wasn't much wider than the Thames at Westminster. Rusty, rotting hulls were sunk into the mud along the opposite shore. An old wooden steamer lay on its side beside a modern, drab green gunboat that bristled with guns fore and aft.

Dug-out canoes were pulled half out of the water on both banks. On an upturned hull beside the bar children took turns at diving into the turbid waters.

We got through two jugs of beer in half an hour: Joel was a man after Bridget's heart, although he was the only one belching, loud and often. Half-Indian half-passing sailor, he turned out to be fluent in six languages and have a fondness for quoting George Bernard Shaw. So much for first appearances.

He tried hard to impress Bridget but his Shavian wit was rather undercut by the blasts of beery breath he belched over her as he spoke.

"It's a cultural thing," I whispered to her as Joel called for another jug of beer.

Bridget ignored me. Nothing new there then. She was busy ogling a half dozen fit-looking Caucasian men huddled at a nearby table drinking beer and talking little.

I braved the wobbly gangplank that led to the lavatory. The lavatory was a rudimentary affair. Very rudimentary: A hole in the floorboards. I looked through it at the foul sludge below.

I recalled visiting my great uncle in a little northern village called Earby when I was a kid. He had a long drop toilet in a shed at the bottom of his garden. It comprised a wooden seat with a hole in the middle fixed above a stream in a ditch some four feet below. The stream ran under each of his neighbor's outhouses in turn.

The foreman who gave my great uncle a hard time in the local factory lived a couple of doors downstream. Once I waited for him to go into his outhouse then I crept into my uncle's, set fire to a crumpled newspaper, and dropped it into the stream where it drifted, blazing, down to the unsuspecting foreman.

I was halfway across the garden before I heard his roar of pain, back in the house before he fell cursing out of the outhouse, trousers round his ankles, one hand on his singed bum.

I was smiling at the memory when I turned to leave and came face to face with the man with the knife.

"Deutsch?" he said.

"No. Sorry."

"Americano?"

"No, sorry. I'm English. And you are …"

"Give me your money or I'll break your face," he said, raising the knife.

"That's not actually correct," I said, without thinking. "I think you mean, 'Give me your money or I'll cut your face.'"

"Give me your money or I'll cut your face."

"That's better," I said weakly.

I stood there for a moment, unsure what to do. I was in a confined space, with no room for maneuver against a knife. Not that I knew how to maneuver against a knife. I thought I'd try trembling instead. It seemed to come naturally.

He took a step towards me and raised the knife higher. I *am* an Englishman abroad, I thought. A certain standard of behavior is expected of me, especially faced with danger. I gave him my wallet. Well, there's no point being a damned fool about it.

He took it, then moved forward again.

He had only taken a couple of steps when another man appeared in the doorway behind him. This man reached round my would-be assailant and grabbed his wrist. The knife clattered to the floor. The next moment the robber went through the rickety wall into the mud below.

I looked at my rescuer. He was from the table Bridget had been ogling. Slim build, neat black hair, bright blue eyes. He held out his hand. My wallet was in it. I took it gingerly.

"Thanks," I said.

"Nice duds but I should go easy on the Armani around here," he said, in a strong London accent.

"You're English," I said. I always state the obvious when I'm in shock.

"Only between you and me," he said, grinning. "And I'm dying for a piss." He walked past me. "If I were you I'd get your little party on the road to wherever you're going."

"We're going to Puerto Naneiro," I said.

The man looked over his shoulder at me.

"That a fact?"

In the taxi back into Leticia I told Bridget what had happened. She seemed unconcerned, but then she was busy trying to get the mud off her Versace trousers.

Back at the travel agency we got Bridget's luggage onto a trolley, which Joel, grunting, pushed down a bustling street. He was almost horizontal, his feet scrabbling for purchase in the mud as he slowly inched the luggage forward. The narrow shops on either side were filled with sacks of produce and racks of hardware. We came to a large pontoon with a bustle of people on it. Skiffs and dug out canoes were moored there. I looked around for our paddle steamer.

Joel took us to a narrow skiff tied up to the barge. I looked down at it blankly. I'd seen bigger boats on the Serpentine. It was about twenty feet long with a crude tarpaulin roof to keep the sun off, a steering wheel at the front, and outboard motor at the back. There was bench seating for maybe six people. A tall, slender man with very long black hair was sitting behind the wheel. He smiled shyly.

Bridget and I swapped quick glances. No time to change into something more *African Queen*. Dressed as we were, we piled Bridget's expensive luggage on a tarpaulin over the puddle in the front of the boat. We sat down. Water slopped around our ankles.

We took off up the river, wreathed in diesel fumes, hammered by the sound of the engine, which vibrated through the boat. Bridget remained silent, her lips pursed. This made me very nervous.

She'd been in a foul mood for the past couple of days, flying off the handle at the slightest thing. Strange expression that isn't it? Why should you be on a handle in the first place?

I focused on the Amazon. It was a surprise. The sun was very hot; it was humid. But the frothy clouds could have been hanging over London and the trees on the banks too looked English. We passed over sluggish brown water threading through impossibly green countryside. Gentle hills succeeded by dense undergrowth. Herons and fisherhawks flapping low across the water.

The canvas roof didn't give much protection from the sun and its reflection off the water as we scudded along. The humidity on the river combined with the smell of the gasoline—and maybe the sight of the river water slopping over her luggage and her Ferragamo shoes—made Bridget feel bad about an hour into the journey.

She was about to vomit over the side when I pointed out that, given the stiff breeze coming from fore, this wouldn't be very polite to Joel, sitting aft. She looked around for something to vomit in, grabbed the first thing that came to hand.

I'm not sure the panama really suited me anyway.

"Can we stop somewhere for a bit," Bridget said to Joel.

Joel suggested we stop at the Indian village we were scheduled to see two days hence.

"I thought it was very remote," I said.

Joel waved his arms at the river.

"You don't think this is remote?"

Just what I needed. Another wise-ass.

Bridget stayed in the boat so I went alone into the Indian village, camera clutched in my sweaty hands, squelching through river mud in my expensive Timberlands, the sun beating down on my bare head. I felt uneasy since I didn't know what the basis of the visit was—were the villagers just exploited objects of tourist curiosity or was there something in it for them?

Joel led me through the village, taking morsels of food from every hut on stilts we passed. The villagers, in grass skirts, were short, pot-bellied, skinny legged, the women with slack breasts and dead black hair tangled down their backs. They were sullen and incurious, unwilling to meet my eye or respond to my greeting. I can't say I blamed them.

A Stone Age tribe, I reasoned, unused to civilization. I looked at the hammocks hung beside the cooking pots in the open huts. A way of life unchanged for centuries. I hated intruding on them like this so I let Joel daub my face with bright orange vegetable dye in "traditional" Indian manner. Oh yeah? At least it raised a titter among my new companions.

One of them thrust a small object into my hand. A dolphin carved out of teak, with quite a wicked-looking forked tail.

"Plenty freshwater dolphin in Amazon, Mr. Nick," Joel said. "See them leaping maybe tomorrow. Sacred to this tribe. Very good carving."

"It's, er, beautiful," I said politely, looking at this smooth piece of wood trying to get some sense of tradition from it.

It was really nothing more than another piece of tourist tat, albeit one made by a Stone Age tribe, but I realized by the way everyone was looking at me that I was expected to buy it.

"Hardwood isn't it?" I said, concerned I would be contributing to the destruction of the rainforest.

"Sure, teak. Last forever."

I agreed to buy it and the Stone Age tribesman led me into his open hut. I had imagined him spending days sitting by the river watching the dolphins and whittling but when I entered his hut I saw not only another three dozen identical dolphins but also a large modern poster featuring a dolphin that had clearly been the model for the one I had in my hand.

When we approached the far end of the village, I noticed one of the younger Indians was wearing football shorts under his grass skirt. Then we came to a football match in progress on a properly marked out, full size football pitch with brilliant white goalposts. The pitch was right next to an enormous satellite dish.

I looked at the dish with disappointment and suspicion. I half expected the voice of the global media tycoon whose paper I was writing a piece for to boom out: "How's the article coming along, Mr. Madrid?"

I trudged back to the boat feeling ridiculous, surreptitiously trying to wipe the gunk off my face. I wiped some on my trousers by mistake. Bridget saw me and smirked. I presented her with the dolphin.

"Too generous," she said, turning it round in her hands then dropping it into her handbag.

After another hour bouncing around on the wide brown waters we approached the small village of Puerto Nineira, the last Colombian outpost on the Amazon.

"I can't see a hotel that looks as if it will have 'Welcome Cocktails,'" I said.

Bridget raised her head from my hat.

"I can't see a hotel at all."

I looked along the flat line of single storey wooden structures. She had a point. The boatman cut the engine and we drifted in to dock at a small bar on stilts jutting out into the river, connected to solid ground by a good twenty yards of rickety-looking planks. A dozen or so soldiers were sitting at plastic tables on plastic chairs, chugging soft drinks from the bottle.

Broad-shouldered, shaven-headed lads in combat fatigues glanced at us blankly. None looked older than twenty.

"We were going to eat here," Joel said, "but because of Mrs. Bridget they will bring the food to the hotel."

"Doesn't the hotel have a restaurant?" I said. According to our itinerary, our hotel was basic. Before, I'd been thinking that if it served cocktails, how basic could it be? Now, I was beginning to wonder.

Joel threw me a pitying glance as he and the boatman began to unload boxes. Then we set off again up the river.

Twenty minutes later we docked at a stump of wood sticking out of the shallows. The bank here was a steep slope some hundred yards long. I looked around for a sign of human habitation, let alone a hotel. All I could see was a muddy track running up the slope with wooden planks at regular intervals.

Leaving the boatman and his assistant to handle the luggage, Joel led us up this muddy track. About fifty yards into our slithering progress we were halted by an enormous dog, barking wildly and jumping around us. It was being friendly in its way. It provided my wrinkled, dye-daubed, sweat-stained £700 suit with the last splashings of mud and slobber it so desperately needed.

At the top of the slope we reached a wooden hut. There were others beyond it in the trees.

"This must be reception," I said to Bridget cheerfully.

"I'll never forgive you for this," she replied, thrusting her head back into my hat.

There was no bow-tied waiter holding a silver tray of cocktails. The hut was a bare room with rough wooden walls and floor and a tin roof. There was a table, three plastic chairs, a dingy sofa, and two hammocks. I could see a kitchen through an open door.

"Not reception then," I said.

"Hammocks?" Bridget snarled.

Joel walked by.

"Hey, Joel," I said. "What's the scoop on those soldiers back at the bar."

Joel turned as half a dozen swarthy men wearing army fatigues, bandanas, and Che Guevera berets came out of the kitchen. Each one carried a machine gun. A man in a bright Hawaiian shirt pushed through them and looked at me coldly.

"The scoop on those soldiers," he said, in a faultless English accent, "is that whilst they are looking for a ruthless guerrilla leader, he has just kidnapped two British journalists."

# TWO

It was Bridget's fault we were in South America. A few months earlier the aptly nicknamed 'Bitch of the Broadsheets' had been abruptly replaced as editor of a Saturday magazine by a young guy who had been, among other things, her protégé.

She got a big pay-off, enough to keep anyone comfortably without work for a couple of years. I gave her six months max.

"I want to go to South America," she said to me. "Why don't you come?"

"Rio?" I said.

"Nah—the real South America."

The thought of Bridget—whose usual axis when she was in the money was Harvey Nicks, Grouchos, and the River Café—hanging out with llamas, looking at Inca remains, and wearing those silly hats with ear flaps in the real South America was one I couldn't easily get a handle on. It made no more sense when she told me she meant Colombia.

"It's the tourist destination of the future," she said.

"We are talking about the Colombia full of murderous guerrillas, ruthless drug barons, out of control militia, corrupt police, shopkeepers putting bounties on street children's lives, other terrible human rights violations, and hopeless government officials?" I said. "That Colombia?"

"That's what the travel pages are saying," Bridget said. "Apparently it's a paradise."

"Bridget, you're a journalist. Since when have you believed what's written in the press?"

We batted it backwards and forwards and the bottom line eventually was that whilst I was willing in principle to go with her to Colombia, I couldn't afford it. Then a PR I knew turned into my fairy godmother—an unlikely event, I know, unless you were a corrupt Tory MP back in the mid-nineties.

Richard Baker was the least likely fairy godmother you'd wish to meet, especially on a dark night. He was big, tough, and ruthless—but then he was in rock 'n' roll public relations. That industry could teach the Emperor Nero a thing or two about being cut-throat.

"How'd you like to cover the Rock Against Drugs Tour?" he said, after the usual chit-chat.

"Music's not really my thing anymore. I'm getting a bit old for it."

"Hardly think thirty-two is over the hill," he protested. "On this tour, you'll be the youngster. Otis Barnes is topping the bill. Plus a bunch of hippies who've done the drugs but are now set on stopping other people having as much fun as they had."

The Late Great Otis Barnes was a name out of my past. Known as the "Late Great," even though he was alive, because his career had been in freefall after a great run of hits through the seventies and eighties.

Drugs and booze had pulled him down, but he'd made a remarkable comeback the year before, knocking that year's bubblegum off the number one perch with "Sinner Man," the song from the film *Confessions*.

The accompanying album had been raved about by just about everybody for its heady mix of blue-eyed soul, jazz, Robert Johnson style blues. and Celtic folk.

"Where's the tour going?" I said.

"Gonna end up doing some stadiums in the States—probably get the usual suspects coming on board to swell the bill then—but the first leg is South America. Brazil, Argentina, Colombia, Peru."

"Colombia? Well, that's very serendipitous—but isn't that something like a death wish version of taking coals to Newcastle? Since most Colombians make their living in some way from drugs I don't think they're going to listen too closely do you? And the drug barons will be really pissed off. Aside from anything else they'll hate the music—they're tango men from way back."

"Yeah, but this tour is funded by Peace International and they want to get the message across to the kids in South America and, presumably, give the drug barons a poke in the eye. There'll be a lot of security."

"So where does it go?"

"After Buenos Aires, Rio, and Brasilia, we do the Bogota National Stadium, onto Peru for Lima and Cusco—wherever the hell that is—and then a big climax in a son et lumiere extravaganza at Machu Picchu, ancient monument on top of a mountain in the Andes. You get the coverage, you can join it where you like."

"Bridget's on at me to go to Colombia. Says it's the next big tourist destination."

"Bridget? How the hell is she? Hey, remember that night in Riga—"

"Only too well," I interrupted. I had known Richard for about three years. Some nine months before he had run a PR trip to Latvia to show off the splendours of the Baltic States to a bunch of journalists who'd pass the news on to their readers, if the journos could remember it when they sobered up.

Riga is a very hip city with a range of tempting alcohols. On this particular night, we'd probably tried them all.

At five the next morning, Richard was attempting to bugger the Latvian national hero in the city center park when Bridget and I saw two angry-looking policemen heading towards him. The buggery was only in jest, you understand—the war hero was a marble statue—but still the two gun-toting rozzers weren't amused.

There were two things the cops in Riga wouldn't stand for: public drunkenness and someone taking the piss out of their country. Richard looked guilty on both counts. The cops had the reputation for hauling ne'er do wells back to the station to beat the living crap out of them. Seeing these two sauntering over, Bridget and I dragged Richard off and we legged it blearily back to our hotel for the start of another rock 'n' roll day.

Now Richard and I sorted out access arrangements and I blagged the commission from one of the broadsheets. I was due to join the tour in Bogota. Bridget and I had flown in a week early but hated Bogota so much we'd got out as fast as we could.

I thought she was going to Cartagena to see an old friend she was being very cagey about so I booked for the Amazon through a slightly dodgy American travel agent. Then at the last minute Bridget insisted on coming along with me.

"I've read about these kidnappings in South America," she whispered as, an hour after our arrival at the wooden hut, we huddled together keeping a wary eye on the guerrilla leader talking to one of his men out on the veranda.

A couple of tough-looking men were leaning back in plastic chairs, another guy at the door had a carbine of some sort laid across his shoulders, his forearms resting on it.

"If your family proves recalcitrant, the kidnap gang start cutting bits off you."

"Considering I don't have any family," I said, shuddering just a tad, "they could have their work, er, cut out with me."

"My mother will get the ransom note then phone her stockbroker to see what her shares are priced at," Bridget said. "Depending on how well they're doing, she *might* pay up."

"It'll be the government they'll approach. They probably don't want money, they want their comrades releasing."

"Ferdinand Porras, at your service," the guerrilla leader said, swaggering over and lowering himself into one of the hammocks. He lay back, his arms stretched above his head. "Wanted by the armies of four South American countries." He looked at me. "Nice suit."

I guess I assumed all guerrillas—pronounced *gueriyas* here in South America—would look like Che Guevera: scuzzy beard, fatigues, beret. This guy was in his Hawaiian shirt, chinos, and bare feet. With manicured toe nails yet. Swept back, lightly-oiled black hair, Spanish good looks—a slight flare of his nostrils and an uptilted chin as he spoke. Saturnine. Definitely saturnine.

"We're in sympathy with your goals," I said.

"Yeah—stop the rainforests," Bridget said.

"*Save* the rainforests," I said, flashing Bridget a look.

"Whatever. I shop at Body Shop. I bought a Lynne Franks' book once."

I stared.

"I didn't say I read it," she said, catching my look.

Porras looked bewildered for a moment, then scratched his head and yawned.

"Kidnapping is a very honorable tradition here in South America," he said. "The guerrillas inherited the practice from the bandidos. When I was growing up I knew many families whose children were kidnapped."

"Their mistake for knowing you?" Bridget said. He glance at her and smiled thinly.

"One family had all four children kidnapped over an eleven year period. Most middle class families send their children away to America or Europe for education not for snobbish reasons but to escape this perpetual threat of kidnap. I myself studied at the London School of Economics."

"That's why your English is so good?" I said, seeing nothing wrong with ingratiation at this point in the proceedings.

"Partly."

"How long will you keep us?" Bridget said in what I could tell she hoped to be an ingratiating voice. It came out sounding like Bette Davis being coy in *Whatever Hapened To Baby Jane.*

"Don't worry," Porras said. "The first generation of guer-rillas used to kidnap people, keep them incommunicado for six months or so, then start lengthy negotiations. But I learned about economics at the LSE.

"I realized it made more sense, that we could increase turn-over, by speeding up the process. Now we reckon to complete every project—that's from initial kidnap through to banking the money—in around three months."

"Three months!" Bridget gawped at him. "I can't possibly stay here for three months." She groaned. "Look I've got places to be. Can't we give a donation or something. My credit card saves dolphins. Take that." She smiled at Porras. "Look, like Nick said, whatever you're against we are, too."

"You mean the exploitation of our natural resources by carpetbagging foreign multinational companies? The destruc-tion of the way of life of our indiginous native tribes? Right wing death squads murdering our children on the streets of our capital?"

"Awful, terrible." Bridget shook her head. When she looked up her eyes were brimming with tears. Bridget moved by other people's suffering? Not exactly.

"I'm supposed to be in New York in two weeks for the

*Vanity Fair* summer party," she said, her voice breaking. "Do you know how hard it is to get an invite?"

I did a double-take. "You didn't tell me about that," I hissed. "How come I'm not your Plus Guest?"

Bridget ignored me and reached out a pleading hand to Porras.

"What if they won't pay?"

"We send a finger or two to persuade them."

Bridget and I both blanched. Porras smiled.

"Has to be done. We want to offer a gold-card service, with added value. If word gets around that we aren't willing to mutilate our clients it gets harder next time."

"But who do you expect to pay for our release?" I said, genuinely puzzled. "I don't have any family and our government isn't exactly going to be rushing to the bank to get the used fivers. It couldn't give a toss."

"Your newspapers. I understand one of you works for one of the richest men in the world and the other for a very prestigious left-wing newspaper. It was my favourite reading when I was a student. Why are you laughing?"

I guess it was the tension. Bridget was rocking in her seat, I was laughing so hard the tears were coming down my face, the sweat rolling down my back.

"We're not staff," I said, gasping for breath, "we're *freelance.*"

He looked puzzled.

"You still have a fiduciary relationship with your newspapers. They still have a responsibility to you."

"Newspaper proprietors probably wouldn't even shell out for a staff writer, given they can replace him or her in a nanosecond," Bridget said. "Britain is crawling with journalism graduates. So there's no way on earth they'd shell out for freelancers."

I nodded my agreement.

"In the ordinary run of things freelancers are treated like

shit. Newspapers take three months minimum to pay us, quibble over expenses, demand full copyright on our articles without paying extra, speak with honeyed words when they need us, don't even return our calls when they don't."

"You got the wrong number, buddy," Bridget said. "You want to make money out of kidnapping journalists you should get an American showbiz writer. They make more in expenses off one article than we make in fees in a year."

Porras scratched his head and opened his mouth to speak, then changed his mind. Instead, he dropped out of the hammock and walked out onto the veranda.

"Well that's done it," Bridget said. "We're either going to be here for ever or we'll be a snack for the local piranha later tonight."

"Joel was telling me piranha get a bad press. They're not nearly as lethal as they're made out, unless you stray into their feeding ground at meal time."

"What happens then?"

"They strip all the flesh off your body in about forty five seconds."

"Where is Joel? D'you think he's in on this?"

Before I could answer Porras came back in. He smiled severely.

"Dinner will be at seven. Until then, please make yourselves at home. Perhaps a beer on the veranda?"

We sat on two red plastic stools on the narrow veranda, looking out across the bend of the river. To the right I could see several tributaries running off into the jungle. I couldn't see the boat we had arrived in.

"At least we might be able to make some money out of this," Bridget said. *The Hostage Years*. My life as a guerrilla leader's moll."

"I think that's more in your line than mine," I said. "But you're right—if we do survive we can expect good coverage in the papers. I can see the stand now: 'Exploring the tributaries of the Amazon River, journalist Nick Madrid and his friend Bridget Frost soon find themselves up the proverbial creek without a paddle.'"

"What makes you think your name would go first?" she said sharply.

The sky darkened and I watched a heron flap towards a tall, broad tree on the bank of the river. As the heron landed on one of the uppermost branches, I saw that there were dozens of other herons with folded wings already settled on the tree. Over the next ten minutes a dozen more found space on there, their distinctive shapes making the tree look like some surreal Christmas tree.

"Isn't that amazing?" I said, transfixed.

"Fucking marvellous," Bridget said, stifling a yawn and peering into her beer bottle to see if there was any alcohol she'd overlooked.

As the sun slipped rapidly below the horizon I thought about Otis Barnes. He'd been in my life, well, almost all my life. My old hippy dad had been a big fan. When he died—he shared Otis's appetite for drink and drugs without sadly his remarkable constitution—I inherited his record collection.

It was enormous, a kind of history of British hip, from early Stax and Atlantic through the real Britpop explosion in the sixties on into British folk and hippy America. Sadly it continued into progressive rock—all the dreadful concept albums and bombast, the Sixties Hammond organ swapped for a Wurlitzer.

But in among them all were the early albums of Otis Barnes. A protégé of hard drinking Scottish folkie Euan Campbell, he started out in the boozy Celtic folk tradition—John Martyn's hard-edged folk-blues rather than Al Stewart's bedsit confessionals.

He played acoustic guitar, of course, and had a wonderful slurry (even when sober) soulful, liquid voice. Hear him, you'd think he was black, especially when he covered Robert Johnson's bad boy Delta blues. He wrote great love songs but live preferred to do harder, rockier numbers and act the beery lout.

He was attractive to women as that most devastating—and most clichéd—of male figures: the romantic tough guy. He'd been a boxer in his teens and had a reputation as a mean street fighter. Quick tempered, he was even quicker to put his fists up. Sadly, he was rumored to use them on his wife as readily as he was in bar brawls.

My thoughts were interrupted by the sight of a dugout canoe appearing on the bend of the river. As I watched the canoeist guide it towards the crude landing post 300 yards beneath us I became aware of someone standing beside me. Porras.

He smiled a wide but evil smile and what he said chilled me despite the heat.

"I should take a little rest for when the sun has gone you will meet your first piranha."

# THREE

Bridget groaned. She was sprawled on a wooden bunk under-neath a mosquito net that looked to be made of Auntie Vi's net curtains. She'd changed out of her red dress. It hung beside my wrecked suit from a nail on the wall. We were both now wearing T-shirts and cotton trousers. I took a swig from a bottle of water I'd picked up in Leticia.

"Guerrillas aren't idealists any more, they're robber barons," she said contemptuously. "They're just after money."

Joel spoke from the floor.

"The universal regard for money is the one hopeful fact in our civilization. Money is the most important thing in the world. It represents health, strength, honor, generosity, and beauty as conspicuously as the want of it represents illness, weakness, disgrace, meanness, and ugliness."

I leaned out of my bunk and looked down at him, lying on his back, his arms folded behind his head, his baseball hat turned to the side. When we had come in off the veranda Joel had been lying in one of the hammocks. He got out and led us down a narrow corridor to this dark bedroom. Bridget had booted him out whilst she changed—quite literally, giving him a vigorous kick up the backside.

His face crinkled into a gap-toothed smile.

"*Man and Superman*—1903," he said.

"I think Shaw was being ironic, Joel."

"What is ironic?"

"Everything these days. Joel, did you tip them off about our arrival?"

"No choice, Mr. Nick," he said without a hint of shame. "They threaten my dearest and nearest." He gestured with a thumb back down river. "One of my women lives in the village you saw. Porras threatened to hurt her unless I helped him."

"And you believed his threats?"

Joel belched unselfconsciously.

"Bad people, Mr. Nick. This man Porras calls himself a connoisseur of cruelty."

"And no money changed hands?" Bridget said.

Joel sat up, gave a nervous little smile.

"Well, sure, a little. Money is the most important thing in the world and all sound and successful personal and national morality—"

Joel yelped as Bridget punched him hard on his ear. He was on his feet and over by the door in moments.

"*The Irrational Knot,* 1905," he called over his shoulder as he disappeared from view.

Bridget sat up on her elbows.

"Lying bastard—he did it entirely for the money."

I nodded glumly.

She surveyed the room then looked over at me.

"You paid to stay here?"

"They said it was basic."

It was like being in someone's garden shed. Rough wooden walls, a roof of layered tree fronds. Mesh at the windows, two broken down bunk beds with thin smelly mattresses and tired sheets. The en suite bathroom was a sink, a showerhead, and a loo in a wooden lean-to across the corridor. Someone had screwed a white china soap dish into the wood in a sad attempt to make it more elegant.

Our conversation was almost drowned out by the sound of the nearby generator that provided the electricity.

"Never imagined the Amazon would be noisier than Shepherds Bush," I said.

Bridget's luggage was piled up in a corner of the room. She opened the top case and drew out a short black dress, a close relation to the red one, cut low at the front and very low at the back. Compared to her usual taste in clothes, this was rather conservative.

She turned and held it in front of her.

"This was going to be my cocktail hour dress. Maybe I'll wear it at dinner, give Porras an eyeful."

"Another eyeful, you mean. I think jeans and a jumper would be more appropriate," I said primly. "You don't want to be giving these guys ideas and I don't want to be defending your honor."

"My knight errant," she said, rummaging in a large vanity case. She brought out hair mousse and hairdryer.

"Also for the cocktail hour."

There was a knock on the door and a young woman in army fatigues and T-shirt came in. She looked no more than nineteen, an Indian girl with long black hair and large brown eyes, taller and slimmer than the Indians I'd seen around here.

"General Porras would like you to join him for dinner," she said, her eyes widening as she saw the red dress hanging from the nail. She started to reach towards it to touch it then remembered where she was and backed out of the room, a faintly embarrassed look on her face.

We went into the main room just as the rain came down, suddenly and hard, hammering on the corrugated roof, drowning out not just the generator but our own voices. Porras was lying on the floor face to face with the dog, whispering endearments and moving his head out of the way each time the animal tried to lick his face.

Porras saw us and got to his feet. He gestured for us to be seated at the rough wooden table. I saw the girl busying herself in the kitchen, her back to us.

"Where's Joel?" I called above the noise of the storm.

Porras shrugged.

"Eating with my men."

I was wondering if I should attempt to overpower Porras—although I hadn't the faintest idea how—when the door from the veranda opened and a young man in oilskins and wellingtons stepped in sideways.

He was carrying a large covered tray. He smiled shyly and bobbed his head before taking the tray into the kitchen. The girl gave him an equally shy smile. The young man came back into the main room and shucked off his oilskins, water puddling on the floor around him. A machine pistol was hanging from a strap round his neck. He seated himself in one of the plastic chairs and apologetically pointed the weapon in our vague direction. His attention, however, was on the girl.

He had brought our dinner. The girl placed before each of us a plate of fried bananas, cassava, and some kind of fish.

"Piranha," Porras said, "caught by my young friend here in your honor."

I was relieved to discover we were going to eat piranha rather than the other way round. I looked at the brightly colored fish on my plate which provoked such fear in the ignorant (i. e. me). It was almost round, some six inches long, with a wide mouth in which I could see the two rows of teeth.

"They don't look much different to teeth in other fish," I said, almost to myself.

"I hate to think what kind of fish and chip shops you frequent in Shepherds Bush," Bridget said, lifting the piranha on her plate with her knife. She examined its underside cautiously. "Since when did you become an expert on fish dentistry anyway?"

Porras said something rapidly in a language I didn't recognize. The girl went over to a large fridge and brought out three beers. She handed them to us.

"How many men do you have?" I said.

"Men and women," he said. "We have no sexism here. Carlita here can kill just as efficiently as any of my men."

Carlita cast us a quick, hard look. I looked down at the grinning piranha on my plate. I wondered if it had fed off any humans lately. The thought that eating it might in some way make me a cannibal made me nauseous. I put my fork down and reached for my beer.

"The number varies," Porras said. "I like to regard my organization as a modern business—we have a mission statement and core values—so I keep the central administration costs down. I out-source a lot of the work."

He indicated the young woman and boy. "Interns. I have a good training scheme. Lots of hands-on experience."

"How hands-on exactly?"

He merely smiled, showing gleaming teeth.

"You're kind of kidnapping plc? We've been hearing of your reputation for cruelty."

"Somebody has speaking out of turn. Tut. This is a cutthroat business and sometimes one has to be literal about that. But I told you, you will not be harmed provided money is forthcoming."

"And if it isn't?"

He speared a piece of banana on his fork and raised it to his mouth. "Let us not spoil our dinner."

My appetite had definitely gone. I took another swig of the beer. Bridget was tucking into the piranha. It had very solid ribs.

"Tell me," Porras said. "Why are you in my country? Are you travel journalists?"

"I'm here to cover the Rock Against Drugs tour when it reaches Bogota next week," I said.

He frowned.

"Really? I am not familiar with this tour—but then in the jungle news is slow in arriving. Who is performing?"

I named the Latin American acts.

"It's a good line-up," he said carefully. "There are some excellent South American jazz musicians performing. I have played with many of them."

"You're a jazz musician? Well, that's great. I love all that South American jazz—Jao Bosco, Ivan Lins …"

"In Britain I performed often with a man called Otis Barnes."

"The Late Great? Well, he's the bloke who's headlining the tour. Big friend of mine, as a matter of fact—"

"He stole my wife."

"—that's to say I met him once. Stole your wife, eh? That's, er, that's—"

"Not quite cricket? You're quite right. And he is in my country? Most interesting." His voice had gone very flat. "Revenge is a dish best eaten cold."

"Is that a saying you have here?"

"No, I heard it in a yankee film about the Mafia—now there's one of the great business successes of the twentieth century. Great branding yet quite diverse—multinational with a portfolio of skills and talents. Managers elsewhere could learn a lot from the Mafia." He shook his head in admiration. "One day maybe."

"Excuse me," Bridget said impatiently. "But shouldn't you be fighting for social justice?"

"You fight for social justice—I want to get rich. You don't think I hang out in the jungle and work these long hours for fun do you? I'm trying to build something for my family."

He got up from the table.

"We're moving from here tomorrow. Back into the jungle.

We'll be having an early start so I suggest you turn in. Oh and sleep with your boots on."

"Why?"

"Vampire bats. They batten on your feet to suck your blood." He saw our faces, gave a cold laugh. "Yes, jungle life—you see why I love my existence here."

The generator turned off at nine. The sudden silence was immediately filled by the chittering of insects and worryingly loud rustling in the roof of our bedroom.

In darkness, with no electricity, the mosquitoes gathered. We scurried into bed under the net curtains. We were taking two kinds of malaria tablets prescribed by our doctors although there was no guarantee that the mosquito that bit you would have the right strain of malaria.

The best thing is to use a good repellent. It didn't take long to discover that the spray I'd bought from the chemist at home wasn't up to the job of tackling malaria's first line troops. The ones that had come inside the net with me attacked with impunity, doubtless sniggering at the effeteness of my protection.

"My mosquito net has a fucking rip in it," Bridget said. "Oh fuck—what's that?"

There had been a sudden pained cry among the rustling and fidgeting coming from the thatched roof above our heads.

"Some predator has got its victim," I said, shining the tiny torch I had with me up at the roof. The thin beam of light was lost in the shadows.

"What do you mean some predator—what kind of predator exactly?"

Snake was the word that came unbidden to my lips.

"Budge over," I said to Bridget, sliding into her bunk.

She turned the torch beam on my face.

"To protect you," I said. I looked down at her. She was wearing a fleece with a hood, pulled tight over her head. My fleece.

"What are you wearing?"

"I'm not taking any chances she said," pulling the hood more firmly over her head.

"You've been rummaging through my luggage."

"Yeah—rather a lot of condoms, aren't there, considering how little success you have with women?"

An Angela Brazil spirit took hold of her and we talked by torchlight for all the world like naughty children in the dorm. Crushed together—the bed was pretty narrow—there were other things for naughty children to do but Bridget and I never had. It was sort of an unwritten rule in our friendship. Maybe that's why we were still friends after all these years.

"I don't know about you but I don't want to spend the next few months sitting here," she said.

"Yeah—mustn't miss the Vanity Fair party."

"I was going to tell you about it."

I shone the torch on her.

"What—afterwards?"

She looked vaguely embarrassed but continued.

"Plus, if we're really going to be hostages we need somebody winsome back home to plead our case and keep us in the public eye—for which read media eye."

"Do you have anyone in mind?"

"I don't do winsome."

"So what are we going to do?"

"Wait until they're shagging?" Bridget said.

I recalled Porras lying on the ground with the slobbery dog.

"Do you know something I don't?" I said.

"The young guy and the girl. I think they'll be our only guards. You must have noticed they've got the hots for each other. If they think we're meek and mild they'll be shagging before the sun's gone down."

# FOUR

Bridget was dead right. We lay pretending to sleep until the young man had checked on us. Ten minutes later we heard giggles, then silence, then gasps, and the gentle creaking of a hammock.

"They're doing it in a hammock?" I said. "Isn't there a joke about that? I get dizzy making love in the normal way."

Bridget looked puzzled.

"Doesn't everybody?" I said weakly.

I slid from the bed and set to work easing the nails holding the netting in place from the windowsill. I pulled back enough of it to allow us to climb through. The moon was remarkably bright, which didn't bode well.

Bridget started pulling her big suitcase towards the window.

"You're not thinking of taking that are you?" I hissed.

"Are you mad? Of course I'm taking it. It's got all my clothes in it. Not to mention my shoes. Well, not all my clothes—thought I'd leave the guerrilla girl the red dress to make up for the trouble she'll be in for letting us escape."

"Am *I* mad? I don't think its customary for escaping hostages to take their luggage with them. It tends to slow you down. Leave it and make a big insurance claim. Just take enough for a couple of days. When the army raid this place they'll find it anyway."

Bridget insisted on taking her vanity case. God knows what

was in it but it weighed a ton. I checked out the door. The noises from the next room were continuing. I was impressed by the boy's stamina—I'm more your five seconds of bliss kind of guy. On a good day, that is.

I climbed out of the window and waited for Bridget. She was preceded by a set of net curtains.

"Bridget?"

"For the mosquitoes."

"You're going to wear it?"

"You have a problem with that?"

"No problem. I just didn't imagine fleeing through the jungle with Miss Haversham carrying her vanity case."

It was at that point someone tapped me on my arm. I jumped three yards.

"Joel—Jesus!"

"Mr. Nick, I'm coming to get you. Need to escape tonight before they move us upriver."

"How did you get away from the soldiers?" Bridget said, dropping from the window in a frothy blur of netting. Joel's eyes widened.

"Miss Bridget, I thought you were Miss Haversham. Charles Dickens a great author. It was the worst of times it was the best of times. Mr. Gradgrind, Tiny Tim."

"Okay thanks, Joel," I hissed. "Shouldn't we be making a move?"

"Follow me," he said, slipping into the trees and heading down the muddy slope to the river.

We followed but lost sight of him after about twenty yards

"Put the bloody torch on, I can't see anything," Bridget whispered.

I shushed her.

"I don't want to see anything, the noises I'm hearing are bad enough."

"Yeah, well I can imagine more when I can only hear."

The jungle was full of noises. Shrieks and cries, the constant rattling and chattering of insects. I'd read of a moth that makes a knocking noise like a woodpecker by beating its wings together. There it was, remarkably loud.

There were also, all around us, the lights of a million fireflies. I added the narrow beam from my torch. It illuminated a fraction of an inch ahead of us, glanced off the eyes of strange creatures. I switched it off quickly.

Joel was waiting for us on the shore.

"They have moored the boat and the dug-out canoe on the other side." He looked uneasily across the broad expanse of water. "We must swim across."

"Are you out of your fucking tree?" Bridget hissed.

"What?" Joel said, frowning. "The boat is over there. We must swim."

"I don't know about you," Bridget whispered fiercely, "but when I hear the word Amazon I think of the word piranha and when I do that I see those scenes in movies where the water boils and a skeleton stripped of all its flesh bobs to the surface. I've seen the teeth buddy. You get my meaning?"

Joel looked from left to right then stepped into the water. It came up to his waist.

"It's a fallacy to think piranha will automatically attack. It's only if you swim in their feeding ground or at certain times of day."

"See," I said. "Told you."

"I must say I'm not reassured."

Joel looked anxiously round. "Or if you're bleeding. Come on Miss Bridget, I assure you that you don't have to worry about piranha at night."

He took another step and I moved unwillingly closer to the water's edge, tugging Bridget along with me.

"Nick, you must be out of your fucking head if you think

I'm going in there. Why can't you bring the boat back over?"

"No paddle. Daren't start engine. Just have to drift with current back to Puerto Nineiro."

I took another step. Joel looked anxiously around then pushed himself forward to breast the water.

"If you're so positive the piranha won't harm us why are you looking so anxious," Bridget called quietly after him as I took my first step into the muddy shallows, pulling her along with me.

"I'm positive you don't have to worry about piranha at night," he threw back over his shoulder as I took my first tentative step into the shallows. "It's the caiman you have to worry about."

I stepped back out, colliding with Bridget in my haste.

"What's a caiman?" Bridget said, her face close to mine.

"An alligator or a crocodile," I said. "I forget which."

"They come out at night," Joel called back nervously. "They lie underwater."

He was some fifteen yards out from the bank now. I could see him clearly in the moonlight.

Bridget and I looked at each other.

"Joel, you go for help—we'll wait here until it arrives."

Joel didn't reply. He kept on swimming, his stroke a combination of doggy paddle and breaststroke. I looked anxiously for anything resembling a log floating towards him.

"In films don't crocodiles hang around on the bank until they see food in the water?" Bridget said, casting equally anxious glances around us. "You see those shots of them sliding into the water and heading for their prey. But if their prey is standing conveniently to hand …"

"Shall we set off through the jungle?" I said nervously, waving my arm and ducking as something brushed past me.

"I didn't realize you'd already been bitten by a rabid bat."

"What's the problem?"

"I mean you're obviously barking. I'm not sure I'd go through the jungle in the day, I certainly won't in the middle of the night."

"It's surprisingly light," I said, looking up at the stars shining brightly. I tilted my head looking for the cluster of stars that made a small question mark.

I had no idea what the formation was called but I'd first seen it as a teenager spending the night on Pendle Hill in Lancashire for Halloween—daft thing to do but I've done stupider things much more recently believe me. Now I always looked for it wherever I was as some sort of comfort.

I found it but it gave no comfort now. A landscape that had seemed curiously English during the day was now transformed into the most alien environment I'd ever encountered—and that included the Fringe Festival in Edinburgh. I'd never felt so far from home.

"I don't think you should make any sudden movements, Nick," Bridget said, looking past me.

"Wha—"

"Trust me on this. That log about ten yards behind you just winked."

"Don't you panic," I said in a deliberately deep reassuring voice.

"Since when did you turn falsetto?" Bridget said. She kept her eyes on the object behind me. "*Are* caiman alligators or crocodiles?"

"What's the difference?" I said nervously, twisting my head to try to see over my shoulder.

"About thirty mph I think. In Florida they can notch up speeds of sixty mph."

"And no traffic cop would dare to pull them over." I turned my head and saw the log-like object some fifteen yards away. "Okay well I think we should climb up the nearest tree here. Don't let him know you're scared. Animals can sense it."

"I don't think these things can be called animals. They're primeval aren't they—Nick, it's moving."

Our speed in getting up the tree from a standing start must have beaten all records, especially as I was still clutching Bridget's vanity case. We stopped some fifteen feet up. The caiman waddled very deliberately over and stopped beneath the tree.

I looked down on it with mounting fear. It was some nine feet long. Bridget was looking down, too.

"They can't climb can they?" Bridget said, hysteria at the edges of her voice.

"Not a chance," I said, trying to sound confident. "Though there is a Caribbean one that can—"

With remarkable suddenness the caiman reared up on its hind legs, held still for a moment, then hurled itself up towards us. It's massive head was suddenly right in front of my face.

"—Jump!" I yelled, rearing back and thrusting the only thing I had—Bridget's vanity case—into its open jaws.

The caiman clamped its jaws shut in some kind of reflex and dropped back to the ground with a juddering thud.

"We are in the Amazon aren't we?" I said, my voice shaking. But when I looked round Bridget had clambered another twelve feet up the tree. I climbed after her.

"Where's my vanity case?" she said accusingly.

I pointed down.

"Oh fuck," Bridget said. "He's got my bloody fags. And my tampons."

"Tampons?" I said. "Is it—are they, er, needed?"

"Will be in a couple of days," she said, halting a few feet higher and wrapping an arm round the trunk of the tree.

"That explains it."

"What?" she said sharply. "Explains what?"

"Nothing," I said quickly. "Absolutely nothing."

I groaned. Bugger the caiman, the chances of surviving the

night with Bridget *sans* fags immediately pre-period were pretty remote.

The caiman jumped again. I'd read the Caribbean caiman could jump six feet into the air to catch its prey. He was short a few feet.

"You're sure they can't climb," Bridget asked shakily.

"Of course they can't, don't be silly."

"Silly? I've just seen one jump six feet in the air, don't tell me I'm being silly."

"Yeah, but would it be jumping if it could climb?"

As I said this the caiman sidled off and slipped quietly into the water.

I wondered what it had heard. I couldn't see the river for the branches of the tree we were in.

"What the fuck is a Caribbean crocodile doing here?" I said.

"Tourist? Extended family? Visiting relatives?"

I looked nervously up into the tree.

"What are you looking for?"

"Nothing," I said.

She glared at me.

"Anaconda—you know, python or boa constrictor—remember we were told the difference when we were in Edinburgh."

I'd had a close encounter with a large python in a flat I was renting the previous year doing the festival. I'd avoided harm. The flat's cat hadn't fared quite so well.

"I mean what are the odds on being menaced by a giant snake twice in a lifetime?" I said.

"What, in the Amazon?" she said sourly, producing an umbrella from the pocket of her jacket. I looked at it in bemusement.

"What you're going to prod it to death? Come on the chances of us climbing up the exact same tree a python is sleeping in—trust me I know about these things."

"As I recall from Edinburgh your knowledge of wildlife is gleaned almost entirely from movies. I'm not sure we can rely on your childhood memories of *The Jungle Book* for an awareness of jungle craft."

I looked back up at my question mark.

"Here," Bridget said, handing me the net curtains. "Otherwise the mosquitoes will bite us to death."

The branch was broad. It was a hardwood tree but quite comfortable. Any other time the noises of the night would have bewitched us—toads, cicadas, the moth that rattled its wings.

In the distance lightning quietly illuminated a heavy bank of clouds. We huddled together against the trunk, the netting wrapped round us.

"You didn't see a marzipan house did you?" Bridget muttered before she fell asleep against my chest.

When I awoke the good news was we hadn't been bitten by too many mosquitoes. The bad news was we were covered in heron shit. I looked up as the last of them flew away, its farewell gift plummeting past me onto the branch below.

It was raining, although under the canopy of the tree we were fairly dry. Well, aside from the humidity.

"So—now what do we do?" I said to Bridget as the sun burst through the trees around us. We looked around. We were as near to the river as it was possible to get. More to the point we were all of 300 yards from the encampment.

"Well, we can't move—they'll find us. We have to stay here until later in the day when help arrives—and if it doesn't then we try to take a boat. With luck they'll think we're miles away."

Half an hour later the young boy ran down the muddy steps to the river bare-chested, machine gun in his hand. He looked across to where the boat Joel had taken should have been at anchor then rushed back up the steps.

Nothing happened after that and the day unrolled into the

longest one of my life. At first it was quite interesting. We saw a school of freshwater dolphin break the surface and leap into the air at regular intervals during the morning.

I was a bit blasé about them—there's a place I go to in Crete to do yoga where the dolphin come right into the bay. I confess to carnal relations with a woman who actually did that most New Age of things and actually swam with dolphins. That's how desperate I can get.

Bridget wasn't blasé, she was totally indifferent. As she was to the birds of all descriptions—fisher hawks swooping down to steal fish from just below the water's surface, herons, pairs of macaws, parrots, oropendula vultures.

We had some water and a couple of melons I'd brought from Leticia. But the tree got increasingly uncomfortable. We spoke little. Even less when a fisherman and his family settled below in a dugout canoe. We couldn't say anything in case they were in cahoots with the guerrillas—though I've never been terribly sure what a cahoot is.

The Amazon teemed with fish, the commonest of which were the dogfish, catfish, and of course the jolly old piranha. Their fishing rods were twigs, their bait bits of fish, from which I deduced they were fishing for piranha.

The fisherman was kneeling in the front, paddling, his wife and two children were behind him. The boat nudged the base of our tree with a hollow thwack.

After an hour of them sitting there Bridget whispered to me.

"I need to go to the loo."

I'd been thinking the same thing. It was hard to see how we could without alerting the fisherfolk to our presence in a rather immediate way. However, I had another reason for not doing. I'd read about a parasitic fish called the candiru. You don't want it to catch you pissing in the Amazon. It travels up your flow of urine then lodges in your urethra. there. It has barbs that make getting it back out virtually impossible—short of amputation that is.

The fisherman and his family moved off around three in the afternoon. They'd caught nothing. We glugged the last of the water. Bridget looked tearful.

"You okay?"

"It's just connections—I finally got my Harvey Nicks card back after the bank manager cut up all my credit cards. It was in my purse in the vanity case."

"Are you saying you don't altogether like it here?"

She didn't answer, just looked around at what I had fondly come to think of as our tree.

"Bottom line—what does your book say about other things we can catch in the ju—what is that?"

As she spoke she grabbed me. An enormous blue moth with the wingspan of a small aeroplane wafted by.

"It's a giant blue moth," I said.

"Is that so-called," she said, grabbing me again, "to distinguish from this one which might be characterized as a smaller—but not much smaller—red moth?"

"You got it."

"Okay—you were saying."

"Well, aside from the mosquitoes carrying who knows how many kinds of malaria, the ants that have already bitten us to death, the vampire bats that can give us rabies, there are chiggers which attack our ankles, some thing that burrows into your skin between your toes and works its way up your bone marrow—yech—then there's—"

"Okay—thanks for the resume. I think we'll leave it there. Well, we have two choices. We can either stay up this tree and starve to death—not to mention suffer poisoning from splinters up my bum—or we can go back to the guerrillas."

"I think they must have gone by now, otherwise we would

have seen them searching for us. And, if they haven't, they'll be pissed at us."

"Yes, but they need us alive and well. But whatever we do, I need to get down from this tree pretty damned fast for an urgent call of nature. I don't know what that diet of piranha, cassava, and fried bananas has done to you but my stomach is churning something terrible."

"Snakes," I said quietly.

"Huh?"

"I'd forgotten snakes, lurking under every bush."

"Waiting for some genteel Englishwoman to lower her bum on them no doubt."

"I can't imagine that would be their idea of a good time. Genteel?"

Bridget ignored me as she shinned—with remarkable dexterity actually—back down the tree. She walked into the low undergrowth, turned, squatted, looked at me.

"Well, come on, you're going to have to keep a lookout for snakes."

"What am I supposed to do if I see one?"

"Hit it with the torch. Step on it. Wrangle it. Anything so long as it doesn't bite me."

Greater love hath no man for a friend than that he shall stand beside her on the lookout for snakes as she squats in the middle of the Amazonas with what shortly turns out to be dysentery.

When she'd finished we moved down to the river's edge and looked across at the dug-out canoe bobbing in the water against the opposite bank.

"You should swim across," she said. "Joel said it's quite safe if it's not feeding time."

"When's feeding time?"

She shrugged.

"Didn't say but the odds must be in your favor."

A dolphin suddenly came out of the water, arced its back, and slid back beneath the surface. It came back out and did a kind of triple jump, with twists.

"I can't imagine dolphin, caiman, and piranha would share the same bit of water can you?" I said.

"If you say so," she said.

"Oh fuck," I said, stepping into the brown water, my foot almost immediately sinking into mud. Taking a deep breath I pushed myself into the water and started to swim.

I didn't make much progress at first, but then doing backstroke with one hand whilst attempting to protect your manliness with your other probably isn't the most effective stroke. After ten yards or so I rolled over—I was so frightened there was scarcely any manliness to protect. I made a mental note to muse on some other occasion on the remarkable mutability of the male genitalia.

Even doing the breaststroke I made fast if splashy progress. I was about halfway across, my body attuned to the slightest ripple of water or stray piece of vegetation when something nudged my side.

I almost drowned there and then. I jerked away from what I imagined to be a caiman's slavering jaws, bicycling my legs as my head went under. When I broke the surface again it was to come eyeball to eyeball with a dolphin.

Just what I needed—a playful dolphin. It nudged me with its long beak again, then slipped under the water, rubbing past my body, and emerging on the other side.

I was trying to figure out if I could hitch a lift on it to the other bank when I heard pops of gunfire coming from the hotel up on the hill. Okay, so the guerrillas hadn't left. The next moment the dolphin ducked under the water again as a motor launch came from nowhere and headed straight for me.

I was about to follow the dolphin's example when a figure in combat fatigues, face daubed in camouflage paint, appeared at the prow of the boat, machine gun in hand, and called out in a familiar voice:

"Got yourselves in a bit of bovver, aintcha?"

# FIVE

Back on shore Bridget was surrounded by half a dozen other men in the same outfits and camouflage gloop. The Cockney who'd rescued me in the toilet back in Leticia and had just now fished me out of the water was talking into a radio handset as the boat headed for the shore. He'd introduced himself as Harry.

Two of the men on shore lifted Bridget into the boat and then followed her in. The leader spoke into a radio microphone and five minutes later a powerful motor launch pulled in beneath our tree.

"So—you guys okay?" Harry said. "Sensible of you to hole up until we found you. All kinds of nasty things in the jungle."

"Like?" Bridget said.

"Pick up hookworm round here really easy, just by walking barefoot on infested earth," one of the other men said. "Down on the shoreline here, lots of sandflies. Some of them carry *cutaneous leishmanias*—gives you a sore that won't heal."

"Then, of course," Harry resumed, "if you're unlucky enough to be bitten by a venomous snake, spider, scorpion, or even river creature you got problems."

"I thought they had serums for all that stuff?" Bridget said.

"Sure they do but they need to know what kind of venom it is. Ideally you got to catch the animal and take it with you for identification."

"Naturally."

"Brave of you to go in the water," Harry said to me. "You didn't piss in it did you? Only there's this fish—"

"I know," I said.

"Swims up the urine—"

"I know—" I said more firmly.

"So did you? Did you piss in the water?"

I looked from him to Bridget and back again.

"Not intentionally," I mumbled. A couple of the other men guffawed. They looked the kind who would. "How did I know the dolphin wasn't a caiman until it came out of the water?"

"Caiman are easy," a brawny, broad-shouldered guy said. "Punch it between the eyes to kill it. Tail meat is very tasty."

"I'll remember that for next time," I said.

Harry laughed, slapped me on the shoulder.

"It's okay mate, the candiru fish wouldn't be able to get through your trousers."

I smiled foolishly.

He offered his hand to Bridget.

"What about my luggage?" she said.

"Was it up at the hotel?" Harry shook his head. "Nothing there now."

Bridget gave me her basilisk stare.

"Fucking great," she said, clambering into the boat. I was, I knew, dead meat.

"All you've got to worry about now is the water you swallowed when you went under. What Puerto Nineira drinks today, seventy-odd communities up the river pissed last week."

I rubbed my stomach and subsided back in my seat. He handed me a flask of water.

"Seem to be forever thanking you," I said.

"You always so danger prone or is it just your lucky week?" he said.

I took a swig of water but said nothing.

"Big bloke like you," he continued, "look like you should be able to look after yourself."

"He does yoga," Bridget said.

"Ah," Harry said, as if that explained everything. I was sure I heard one of the other men mutter, "Powder puff."

"What are you guys—SAS?"

"That would be telling wouldn't it?" Harry said.

"Secret mission, huh?" I knew the SAS were flown in to rescue British hostages all the time over here. They were advisers on the siege in Lima when the Tupac Amaru held all the guests at some shindig at the Japanese embassy hostage. I also knew they'd been used to help fight the drug cartels. "You're chasing the drug barons or the guerrillas?"

"We're not here," Harry said levelly. "You never saw us. And I wouldn't advise you to go round saying the SAS were operating here."

It was kind of a threat and whilst I'm not quite the pacifist Bridget was suggesting by saying I did yoga, as if there were an automatic link—actually, the yoga I do is quite vigorous, thank you very much—I wasn't into macho stuff.

Besides, I'd seen a TV documentary once where an SAS man was explaining how he got out of trouble if he was in bother in a pub—"I'd bite the guys nose off. That usually does the trick." I imagine it would.

"Did Joel come and get you?"

The leader nodded slowly.

"In a manner of speaking."

His radio crackled into life and he moved to the front of the boat, speaking quietly into it.

We pulled in at Puerto Nineira. I'd been wondering what Harry had meant by his "In a manner of speaking" about Joel. When I saw his boat docked at the bar with a tarpaulin over something lying in the prow I realized what he meant.

Harry nodded when I gave him a questioning look.

"Boat drifted down here. The soldiers found it."

Bridget and I made to cross over into Joel's boat. Harry motioned us back.

"You don't want to see. He had his throat cut. Almost took his head off."

I swallowed.

"Where are the soldiers now?" Bridget said.

"Back at base. British hostages not something they want to get mixed up in," Harry said. "They tipped us the word. Nice life they've got. No real danger from either guerrillas or drug barons. But there is some drug activity here—somewhere in the middle of the jungle are all the drug refining factories."

"And that's why you're here?" I persisted.

"Leave it out, will ya?" he said. "I told you—we ain't 'ere—okay?"

"What happened to the guerrillas?"

"Not the kind of question to ask in polite society, Nick," Harry said.

"There was a young couple," I said.

"I should leave it, son," he said, fixing me with a cold blue stare.

"No, we want to know," Bridget said.

"Usual rules of engagement darling. They fired on us, we returned fire."

"They're all dead?"

"Couple. The rest melted away into the jungle, as you might say." He held our look. "Don't be too grateful we got you out now willya?"

It was a four-hour trip down to Leticia. The humidity was intense but I didn't realize it until we slowed and the breeze lessened and I immediately started to leak water.

Halfway through the journey the men changed into civilian clothes and stowed their weapons in sports bags.

We moored at the same pier as before. They escorted us back up the dusty main street to the main hotel. Over a beer Harry explained our options. Or rather, lack of them.

"I don't know how long you were planning to be down here. But if I were you I'd go back to Bogota on the next flight. There's a room here at your disposal. We've put your luggage in there. You got your passports and stuff? Okay, you got about an hour before you need to go to the airport. Then I'd get the hell out to the U. S. or Britain."

"We were supposed to be down here for a week," I said.

"Nix that. You were targeted and, for all I know, you may still be targeted." He paused. "We didn't get Porras. We think he did for your guide then took off. Listen—he didn't give you any indication as to his next destination did he?"

"He said he was taking us farther into the jungle. But who exactly did you get? Did you get the girl?"

"Look. it's not something I should be discussing but no, there was no girl. That's all I'm going to say."

"I can't leave South America," I said. "I'm here working for the next month."

"In the Amazonas?"

I shook my head.

"Well, at least get the hell out of the Amazonas. Then get a *vacuna*."

"A vaccination?"

"Sure. It's like insurance. You buy one direct from the the kidnappers—it protects you from being kidnapped because you've already paid them."

"How much?"

"Okay for $100,000 you get maybe protection from a $1 million kidnap."

"Wouldn't it be cheaper just to hire you guys to protect us?"

"We're not in K & R."

"K & R? I think I need a full time translator here."

"Kidnap and ransom or kidnap and rescue depending on who you're talking to."

"That's what you do?"

"Nah. Bunch of ex-spooks do all that. Colombia keeps 'em busy."

"Okay." I thought for a moment. "What about the authorities? Shouldn't they be told what happened?"

"Sure we can do that—if you want to be tied up in red tape for the next month and be kept confined to barracks—probably literally—'til things get sorted out—but I tell you, sometimes round here it's best to do things kind of informally. There's a guy at the British embassy I'll put you in touch with. He'll debrief you but he'll keep it quiet."

We showered and in the privacy of the bathroom. I checked as best I could I didn't have a fish stuck up my Y-fronts.

Harry, in T-shirt and chinos looking every inch the tourist, dropped us at the airport. He stopped ten yards beyond a drunk lying flat on his stomach on the pavement. People were stepping round and over him. He'd been rolled, his trouser pockets pulled out.

"Shouldn't we do something?" I asked.

"Just keep on walking," Harry said through the car window. "He's the customs guy who found the consignment of drugs the other day. He's not someone you want to be standing next to in the immediate future."

He held his hand up in a little wave.

"Okay friends—"

"Thanks for all your help," I said.

"No problemo—and in fact I'd rather you forgot all about it and me—forget we even exist."

We took the next flight out. Looking out of the window at the rainforest spread out below me as far as the horizon, the Amazon threading through it, I sighed with relief.

"I think I'm more your villa in Umbria type when it comes right down to it," I said to Bridget.

She too was looking out of the window.

"We're going to lose money on this you know," she said. "I can't imagine our insurance covers kidnapping and I don't think that spivvy yank will refund the cost of the unused part of our holiday, do you?"

"What do you want to do when we get back to Bogota? I've got three days before I'm due to join the tour. We could go up to Cartagena to see your friend."

"Meet the rest of the jumping Caribbean caiman family? No thanks."

"Who is this friend you're being so mysterious about?"

"None of your business," she said.

Bridget's attitude puzzled me—hurt me, too. We'd never had any secrets from each other before, except for things I was really ashamed of that is. But she wasn't to be drawn.

"I think Harry and his friends were mercenaries," she said in a transparent attempt to change the subject. I let her off the hook.

"Mercenaries or SAS, what's the difference?" I said. "They're up against the drug barons I guess."

"Nice ass," she said before putting on her headphones for the in-flight movie.

Bogota isn't anybody's idea of a tourist town. Sprawling, polluted, with pot-hole roads and the most terrible slums alongside huge chrome and glass skyscrapers. Much of it comprises no-go areas for the tourists foolish enough to have believed the supplements and gone there in the first place.

We had booked into the hotel the tour would be staying at. We were on the first floor in adjoining rooms. The lift was slow so Bridget and I walked up the flight of stairs. We stopped twice to catch our breath.

The problems of altitude in Bogota had taken me by surprise. We were 2,650 meters above sea level. At that altitude air pressure is lower so each lungful of air captures fewer oxygen molecules. I assumed that with my yoga and all the breathing exercises I did I would scarcely notice.

How wrong could I be? A couple of minutes exertion and if I didn't stop immediately I'd feel dizzy as well as rubber-legged.

"This could kill your sex-life stone dead, Nick," Bridget gasped as we had made our slow progress to our adjoining rooms. "I mean you find it difficult to survive more than a few minutes shagging as it is. Imagine if you couldn't get your breath on top of that."

I didn't respond to her cheap joke, partly because I wondered who'd been blabbing, largely because I'd been thinking the same thing. I followed Bridget into her room. She'd sent it on whilst we set off for the Amazon so the rest of her luggage was piled in here.

Bridget was one of the last surviving travel divas, the kind that didn't think a girl could go anywhere without thirty-five items of luggage. The startling thing was that for a woman with so many clothes she could always look so dire.

Playing the percentages there were obviously times when she looked okay but most of the time she looked like an expensive dog's dinner, leather and suede in bright colors and startling lengths combining to make her look like an expensive bag lady.

There were bags of Colombian coffee on top of the television. We'd brought them into the country with us. Bridget had been told by a friend in London that you can't get a decent cup of coffee in the whole country because all the best stuff is exported. I'd been worried about customs—how mad would they think we were?

I stood by Bridget's window and looked across at the hills beyond the wide highway. They were covered with wooden huts and other shelters cobbled together from cardboard, plastic sheets, and odd bits of tin. They were hovels of the most basic sort, leaning at odd angles or half collapsed.

Beside them were these elaborate skyscrapers and apartment blocks - chrome and glass, expensive brick, lush hanging gardens.

"All paid for by drug money," I said when Bridget joined me and handed me a glass of wine. "There's so much money from drugs awash in this country they can't figure out enough ways to launder it. Fifty percent of the money circulating in Colombia is being laundered one way or another. All building in Bogota is drug-related. A place like this must be so deeply corrupt you assume everyone is on the take."

We'd arranged to meet Harry's embassy contact at some club near the Presidential palace. We decided to walk. Okay, I decided to walk. Unwillingly Bridget swapped her five-inch heels for a pair of trainers.

Within minutes of leaving the hotel we came to an army barracks, bang in the middle of the city. A row of tanks lined up on the square, guns pointing outwards. A tank either side of the entrance. Blank-faced young soldiers in puttees and polished boots, machine guns at the ready.

In the shopping area every shop had a guard, most of them armed. We saw a heavily armed guard—pistol at each hip, rifle at his side—giving fierce looks to the passers-by. He was guarding a dry cleaner's.

"I read that when the drug people moved in on the coast in Cartagena they were very generous in what they paid people for their houses," I continued. "Then they went back later, said they had overpaid and demanded their money back. People had no alternative to selling of course.

"You'd get a visit from a man who'd say he was going to buy your house. You'd say, 'But it isn't for sale.' He'd say 'You don't understand—I want to buy your house. It's an order not a request.'"

The rain came, sudden and hard. We dashed for the nearest doorway. We sheltered in the shop doorway and within five minutes a startling thing happened. The subterranean life of Bogota was pushing to get out. Sewers overflowed into the gutters, the gutters overflowed onto roads and pavements. I looked beyond the road to the hillsides packed with the shanty towns. Flash floods were running down the slopes, taking debris and garbage and the odd shelter with them.

I was stunned by its immediacy. I watched in fascination as a heavy manhole cover in the middle of the road seemed like the lid on a simmering pan, bubbling beneath the pressure of who knows what disgusting stuff.

The rain showed no sign of letting up. Our destination was only a couple of streets away. We were soaked by the time we got there. It was some kind of club. We pushed open the doors and went into a dimly lit foyer.

We could hear a miked-up voice in the next room but not what it was saying. Then muffled applause. We went into a small room with a very small stage at the far end. A good crowd was sitting at tables with cocktails and beers.

"Sorry mate, private party," a little man in an oversized jacket said in a low voice as he stepped in front of us to bar our way.

"Didn't expect to hear a Burnley accent in Bogota," I said. "I'm from Ramsbottom myself."

"Tupp's Arse by God," the man said, taking me by the arm. "You must be Nick and Bridget. I'm Ernest Beacon. I'm afraid you've just missed the show."

"Tupp's Arse?" Bridget said with a curl of her lip. "Is this some kind of code you're speaking in? I thought you told me you came from Manchester."

"Near Manchester," I said. "What show?"

"It were a right belter, too," Ernest said, ushering us to a table. He was in his mid-forties, I judged, receding hair, round face, stocky build. He had on a jacket made of some really odd material. He caught me looking at it, leaned towards me.

"Feel that lapel. Go on."

I reached out and rubbed the lapel between my fingers. I frowned.

"Deckchair material?"

"Feels like it doesn't it?" he said, sitting back.

He looked around the room.

"All ex-pats," he said. "Pretty lively bunch of engineers from the oil industry." He pointed at a tall overweight man sitting beside a nervy woman in a black velvet cocktail dress that was as ill-fitting as Ernest's jacket.

"He's the head of a big airline's South American operation. That's his wife, Myrtle—hardly ever leaves her house and certainly never the city because she's terrified of being kidnapped. See her dress? That's a bulletproof dress she's wearing. Like my jacket.

"Bulletproof clothing is very fashionable in Colombia this year, everybody is that terrified of death or kidnapping. That dress and my jacket can handle 32 calibre, 38 calibre, and 9 mm pistol—even an Uzi."

"What's it made of?"

"Christ knows—some compound five times stronger than steel. Hangs a bit loose at first but Myrtle tells me with her dress body heat moulds it round her breasts—"

He looked at Bridget, no slacker in lung development, and got flustered.

"They can bulletproof anything these days," he concluded weakly.

"You're used to dealing with kidnapping?" I said.

"In Colombia kidnapping is endemic. And there's nothing you can really do about it. Kidnapping is almost a national past time. Thousands of people, including dozens of multinational executives, are snatched every year. Some focus on fast food kidnappings—snatching some shopkeeper and giving him back pronto for a small ransom. You were very lucky. Usually if you're targeted, that's it, however much security you have. There's a whole K & R industry here. You know about K & R?"

"Thanks to this experience."

"Well, K & R is big business but it does nothing in the way of prevention. The K & R professionals give advice to newly arriving corporates—basically it boils down to *don't get noticed*. But really the K & R set-up is designed to do the business after a kidnapping. The job of the professionals is to get you back out alive. Provided you're insured with them."

"So K & R is a kidnap insurance deal? How much does it cost?"

"Conventional plan costs anywhere from $10,000 to $150,000 per person per year. Or you can buy a *vacuna*—you know about those?"

"I know," I said.

"What expats have to get used to here—and often can't - is the stockade life. Living in a secure area, guards outside your house, guards inside your house. Bars on the windows, locked gates everywhere.

"You should see Myrtle and George's bathroom. The walls are machine-gun proof. The door is bomb-proof—steel, set in a steel doorframe, huge iron bolts—the works." He sniggered suddenly, showing long, yellow teeth. "If you're taken short and there's someone already in there—you just have to wait your turn."

I smiled politely. Bridget's mouth twitched, which counted as far as she was concerned.

"The cost of preventing kidnapping is often higher than the ransom would be," he went on. "Myrtle and her husband are driven round in a Mercedes that's like something out of James Bond. It's bomb and rifle proof, has flip down gun portholes, and you can release an oil slick to throw off your pursuers."

He leaned forward and whispered: "Don't tell them I told you but they both have homing devices implanted in their bodies." He sat back again. "But what's the alternative—there are thousands of kidnaps here a year and that means thousands of deployments, thousands of settlements."

"As in?" I said, unfamiliar with the lingo.

"Sorry, it's the language we ex- Scotland Yard people use."

It worried me that Ernie—excuse me Ernest—could be ex-Scotland Yard but then I've got a modern view of the way sleuths should work. It certainly didn't involve language.

"A negotiation is a deployment, a ransom is a settlement," he explained. "It's a game over here—though a pretty serious one. But the same gangs negotiate with the same kidnap negotiators. Porras is known to most of them—first name terms.

"You are in probably the most violent society in the world—drive by murders, kidnaps at traffic lights or road junctions, civil war."

"Do the kidnappers ever get caught?"

"Some, but only about 1 percent ever get convicted. More likely they'll be executed on the way to the police station."

"So these kidnap negotiators—"

"Have an 85 percent success rate with people that are insured with them. Their first rule is Preserve the Porcelain: keep the victim alive. The kidnappers want that, too. Although kidnappers have tried to ransom dead bodies, they know they get more money if the kidnapped person is alive."

I swallowed.

"Sounds like we were lucky."

"Damned lucky. It's usually not a good idea to send in the men with knives in their mouths—too risky—or to involve the police since so many are on the take but Harry and his team were around at just the right time."

"Why were they around? Who are they?"

"The Colombian government has these stupid laws to try to sort out the kidnapping problem—kidnap insurance and negotiating with kidnappers is forbidden. Of course everybody ignores the rules but it means, in effect, that you are breaking Colombian law."

"And Harry is who?" I repeated.

"Best you don't know that. That's why I'm debriefing you here rather than at the embassy. I'd like this to remain unofficial, just as Harry is unofficial."

"But he's working for the British government?" Bridget said.

"Negative."

Ernest brought out a business card.

"You've got my home number there. If you see Porras again or if you think you're in danger—call me day or night. You understand—day or night."

I looked at him. He seemed remarkably relaxed for a man who spent every day under the threat of kidnap, possibly death.

"How do you find a life for yourself here?"

He smiled almost shyly.

"Magic."

"What—pulling rabbits out of hats?"

"Have you read any Gabriel Garcia Marquez?"

"Who?" Bridget said. If it wasn't in *Vogue* or—grrr—*Vanity Fair*, Bridget wasn't interested.

"Sure," I said, not sure why Ernest had asked.

"He's known as a magical realist but he's also Colombian. The world he describes—that mixture of magic and harshness, beauty and cruelty—isn't imaginary, it's Colombia. There are many things that are beautiful about this country and these people."

Bridget at least tried to stifle her yawn.

As we were leaving I asked again: "What is this place?"

"The Bogota Magic Circle—we meet every Thursday. Come along if you're in Bogota next week."

When we went back outside the rain had stopped but the air was sultry and smelled bad, the heavy clouds trapping the pollution in the city. We walked back as briskly as breath permitted to the hotel. When the sun was shining it was very hot but otherwise it was a constant chilly spring day in the city.

As we turned the corner onto the street of our hotel I saw a solid-looking Mercedes draw to a halt out in front. I watched as a big man climbed out and staggered across to the hotel entrance. He stumbled on the three narrow steps before the door then pushed his way into the foyer.

I recognized the drunk—for drunk he certainly was. It was Otis Barnes.

# SIX

Bridget went to her room to catch up on some sleep. I sat in the bar with a glass of wine and thought about Otis Barnes.

He got into drugs in a big way in the late seventies and his music went ethereal. He produced some beautiful, spacey ballads. This was around 1978 just as I was getting into punk but I went with my dad to a couple of gigs. Otis would sit there alone in a spotlight and just lose himself in the long drawn out notes, the slurred vocals, the bent chords.

I guess this is the time he and his wife were splitting. It was hypnotic, soulful, and hopelessly sad.

I got into punk—yeah, well, we all make mistakes—then came out of it and my dad died soon after. Otis Barnes released an album of soulful, jazzy, polyrhythmic stuff, all held together with that breathy, growling vocal. He did covers of a couple of swoony old fifties songs that got him in the charts as a late night lover man.

I bought the albums through the eighties, interviewed him a couple of times when I first started out as a music journalist. He had a couple more chart hits, especially with his ballads. Performed live with a great brass section.

Then his second wife left him—rumors of more brutality at home—and he kind of fell apart. He was in such agony—self-pity sure but still tragic to see—that making his next album he kept breaking down. It was such a sorrowful experience and such a sorrowful album the record label boss who was his friend refused to release it. Barnes was a complex character—the depth of his tenderness in his love songs was intimately related to his capacity for violence.

The album, brilliant, unremitting, sorrowful remained on the shelf for two years. It was finally released and produced a mega-hit single with "Never Leave Your Lover Man" but Otis was in no condition to tour or promote either the single of the album. He still found it too painful to sing the stuff. So, he missed the boat.

Since then Otis Barnes had been losing his battle with drugs and booze whilst producing the odd album with a couple of good tracks and the rest fillers. He'd switched record labels a few times, presumably because his reputation for being more difficult than brilliant these days (the delicate balance had tilted the other way) made him more of a liability than an asset.

Then, almost miraculously, he turned himself around. Maybe it was the love of a new woman, maybe it was that he finally exorcised his demons by facing them.

For years he'd had a morbid obsession with James Hogg's novel, *Confessions of A Justified Sinner*, in which the devil in human guise, the guise of a friend, lures the main protagonist into committing more and more lurid crimes.

The two outstanding tracks were both inspired by the James Hogg book—a self loathing song called "Sinner Man" and one about betrayal called "Dark Friend."

They were the best songs based on a book since Sting was inspired by Anne Rice's *Interview With A Vampire* to write "Moon Over Bourbon Street." But they might not have reached a wider audience had they not come to the attention of film director Julian Parkinson who was making *Confessions,* a Hollywood version of the book, starring Alice Denver, trying to prove she could act.

Julian used both tracks, one to open, one to close the film. The soundtrack album was released long before the film as part of the marketing plan. The film bombed—nobody wanted to see an unsmiling Alice Denver—but the soundtrack album was a big success. Suddenly Otis Barnes had himself a best-selling album and a number one hit with "Sinner Man."

And this time he had his shit together. He went into some expensive detox place in Sussex, got off the drugs and booze, shed a couple of stone, and, age fifty, became a fervent and outspoken anti-drugs guy, roped in to head the Rock Against Drugs tour, cleaned up, in love, on form, the bad living a thing of the past.

Which is why it had come as a bit of a surprise to see him dead drunk at the hotel. And to see that he didn't look much better at the subsequent press conference.

The room was full of journalists, a couple of TV crews, and a heavy swathe of security people. I sat off to one side with a view down the corridor along which the rock stars would come.

So it was that I saw them advance, surrounded by yes-men, assistants, agents, and managers. I saw Richard whispering urgently in Otis Barnes's ear, Otis thickly nod, Otis lean on Richard as he tried not to stagger.

He was a big guy and, apart from the fact he couldn't stand up straight, in good shape. He'd obviously been working out. He looked trim—and tough. He had black tousled hair and a full black beard. There was a coarseness to his face and something dangerous about him. Not the kind of guy you'd want to cross—I'd heard stories of him holding bookers up by their ankles to shake the money out of them when they tried to get away without paying him.

Slumped behind the desk and its jumble of microphones, his eyes hidden behind wraparound shades, Otis could get away with it for a while. Occasionally, his head swivelled slowly from side to side, a benevolent smile on his face, as if he were blessing the assembled throng. I half expected him to stretch out his hands in a benediction.

After the preliminary statements by the representatives of Green Power, the rock stars were introduced—aside from Otis they included the lead performers from the jazz sextet The Joe Blows and the hippy-dippy Fertile Lands.

On the whole, the journalists' grasp of English was very good—more foreign educated kidnap risks presumably. There first few questions were about drugs then a plump woman in stiletto heels sitting in the front row put up her hand.

"I have a question for Otis Barnes." She had a lot of teeth and long crimson nails. Otis moved his head a fraction, possibly in response, possibly not.

"When last did you cry—and why?"

There were smiles, a little tittering from the stage and the journalists in the body of the room. All eyes were on Otis. Was he awake behind those glasses? Functioning? I saw Richard's smile become a rictus as the seconds ticked by and Otis made no response. Eventually, cautiously, Otis leaned towards the microphone. He smiled benignly.

"When I got my last bank statement," he growled. Everyone laughed. Richard looked relieved but it was clear the woman was waiting for a proper answer. Otis was aware of it, too.

"Getting off the drugs was pretty horrendous for me," he continued. "I certainly cried then. I raved, raged, and ranted, yeah, but I cried, too."

"Was it cold turkey?" the woman said, delivering the phrase hesitantly.

"More cold chicken, actually," Otis said. "It was a place

in the Home Counties and they were very good on using leftovers."

This passed the South Americans by, although the other musicians had a quick snigger. The questions rolled away—the usual what are your songs about stuff. Otis hadn't sounded particularly drunk, given that he was known for slurring his words anyway.

Another journalist asked him a question.

"You want your album to say something?"

"Yeah, I want it to say, 'Here's the money for that yacht you wanted.'"

People laughed. The woman in the front row, a flirtatious lilt to her voice, said:

"I have another question for Otis. What does he think of South American women?"

Otis sat back in his chair and spread his hands out.

"I would have thought that was obvious since for the past three months I've been shagging the arse off your Queen of Salsa."

"Shagging?" the woman said to her nextdoor neighbor. "*Come* shagging?"

Conchita Esperanza, the Queen of Salsa, was Colombia's most popular singer, danced to in salsa clubs around the world. If the British tabloids were to be believed—no sniggering at the back there—Otis and Conchita had indeed been making the beast with two backs of late.

Richard was still grinning his shit-eating grin. Definitely a rictus. There was some embarrassed laughter then a kind of hiss and a stamping of feet started at the back of the room and carried in a wave through to the front.

The first death threat arrived within the hour.

"Richard!"

"Nick!"

"Richard!"

"Nick!"

We both stood grinning, expectant, each waiting for the other to progress the conversation since with many PRs that exchange *is* the conversation (with, if you want to get flowery, the occasional "How are you?" "Fine how are you?" added).

Richard was ten years younger than me, a beefy good looking longhaired man brimming with confidence—on occasion too loud, great singing voice, big hit with the women. In Riga he made even Bridget seem staid. He was pushy and he was a success at what he did. This tour was probably the biggest of his career, since he had the dual role of PR guy and tour manager.

We were standing in the bar of the hotel an hour or so after the press conference.

"So how's it going? Had a bit of a shock at the press conference seeing the state of Otis."

"Yeah you thought he was drunk right. No fucking way. Can you believe this bloody altitude. Christ I walk ten yards I got to stop for breath."

"Nice attitude to women," I said. "Very chivalrous."

"He was under the weather."

"He was almost under the table—he was drunk, Richard."

"Strike that. He had altitude sickness. He wasn't aware of what he was saying. He was misquoted." Richard sighed, a sigh far too worldly for one so young. "Whatever excuse you want."

"Why'd he fall off the wagon?"

"Conchita tried to chop off his johnson."

"Wha—"

"Not for the first time."

"Because?"

"He'd slept with some ambitious female music journalist."

Richard looked at me and grinned.

"Not for the first time," we said together.

"So how is it going?" I repeated.

"You mean aside from the usual horrors of dealing with rock stars, rock stars managers, groupies, roadies, all the paraphernalia of a major tour, and my giant ego? Like a dream."

He chuckled.

"Course there are one or two slight hiccups but thank the gods they're Horace's problems not mine."

"Horace?"

"Otis's manager—yeah I know, don't get many Horaces in rock 'n' roll—at least any who'll own up to the name."

"Problems aside from the demon barber of Bogota? Like what?"

"His ex-wife, Mara, is in Fertile Lands."

"Get out!"

"The bass player from his old band, the one who's suing him claiming to have co-written 'Lover Man,' is in another act on the bill." Richard chuckled and shook his head. "Don't be put off by Otis's asshole remark this morning. He likes to shock and sometimes he doesn't quite judge it right."

"I'd say."

"He's quite a character. You should hear some of his stories. You will hear some of his stories."

I shrugged.

"We'll see. How're you handling the drugs thing. I seem to recall you're quite partial to a toot on a regular basis. How are you handling abstinence?"

Richard gave me a wolfish grin.

"Ways and means, my man. Ways and means." He nudged me. "You hear about the plane coming in from Rio. Someone had stashed 600 kilo of cocaine in steerage. Cheeky or what?

Held us up for hours. They use the presidential jet and navy vessels, too, you know."

I was telling him about the kidnap ordeal when a big black guy shouldered his way into the room. A very big black guy. About my height—6'4"—but all muscle. He moved easily though.

"I didn't like the way this guy Porras was talking about Otis. Seemed like he had a score to settle."

"He'd better get to the back of the queue—" Richard spotted the black man walking by and jumped to his feet. "Hey, bro," he said, clapping him on the arm. "Nick, this is Ralph, the tour's security manager, tell him about this guy Porras."

Ralph looked down at Richard, clenched his jaw.

"I ain't your bro," he said with such intensity Richard moved back a couple of steps. "So don't hit me with that homeboy shit."

"Hey, man—" Richard said.

"Hey nothing," Ralph said. "I get so fucking weary of this street shuck. I'm black but I was brought up on the upper west side. My father is a lawyer. I studied classical trumpet for a higher diploma. I'll take Wynton Marsalis over rap any day. I'm the size I am not because I was too dumb to do anything but lift weights for five hours a day at the neighborhood gym but because I was an athlete as well as a musician at college. A swimmer. I'm sorry I'm not a sprinter but there it is."

Ralph's fierce stare raked across me as well as Richard, then he walked off. Richard watched him go.

"But you're still a glorified bouncer, Ralph," he muttered. "What you got to say to that, huh?" He shrugged. "Guy's kinda wired."

I watched the big man circle the room. He moved well for one so big. Unable to find who he was looking for he glided from the room.

"Good taste in music though," I said as I saw Bridget pass Ralph coming through the door, crane her head back round to get another look at him, then sashayed into the bar trailing, for reasons best known to herself, a long silk scarf, the kind I always associated with Isadora Duncan getting strangled.

"Bridget!"

"Richard!"

"Bridget!"

Yeah, well, you can fill in the rest for yourself—see above and factor in a few air-kisses followed by a big hug.

"You coming to the concert tomorrow, doll?" Richard said.

Any ordinary Joe called Bridget "doll" and the next time you saw her she'd be using his scrotum as a tobacco pouch. For Richard she merely smiled a girlish smile. It was nauseating.

I idly wondered if they'd made the beast with two backs in Riga. Bridget didn't really go for men younger than her—well, unless, like Richard, they were really dishy.

"No, I'm flying up to Cartagena to see an old friend," she said.

"Cool place," Richard said. "Watch out for the crocodiles though. I saw a thing on telly once—apparently they can ju—"

"We know," I said. "We met one in the Amazon."

"Missed his stop had he? How come?"

"Let's go out and get a drink somewhere, we'll tell you all about it," I said.

We walked slowly through the old town, down narrow, dusty streets. Young soldiers with high-cheekboned Indian faces wearing green fatigues hoisting automatic rifles were loitering on each street corner—we were fairly near the presidential palace by now.

We climbed half a dozen steps onto the terrace of a cafe and I had to stop to catch my breath. When we sat down I ordered a fruit pulp drink.

Bridget and Richard both ordered large vodka and tonics.

"You're not supposed to drink alcohol until you get acclim—"

Bridget gave me a look that made me think tobacco pouches.

"—nothing absolutely nothing. But I certainly don't want to get altitude sickness."

"What're the symptoms?" Richard said, taking a big swig from his drink.

"Shortness of breath, headache, pounding heart, giddiness, insomnia, maybe vomiting."

"And here I just thought I was in love," Bridget said with a quick laugh.

"Don't laugh," I said primly. "Sorocha or hypoxia—they're the technical terms for altitude sickness—are hard to shake off. And you've got to watch the dehydration—apparently occurs very rapidly at high altitudes. But sip don't slurp—altitude, exertion, and excess fluid can lead to high blood pressure."

"How come you know all this shit?" Richard said.

"I like to do my research," I said, preening slightly.

"He's a swot," Bridget said.

"Varicose veins, hemorrhoids, and other vascular conditions are often irritated by high altitudes."

"Yeah, yeah."

We told Richard about the kidnap.

"So the sooner we can get out of Colombia the better."

"You can't want to leave Bogota," he said. "Great city. Enlightened too—on Sunday they close the roads for rollerbladers and cyclists—that's thoughtful."

"If you're a rollerblader or a cyclist. I've read about that—they only do it because the President's son is a keen rollerblader—sorry it still doesn't mean Bogota is my idea of a tourist town."

"Bogota isn't anyone's idea of a tourist town. Everywhere

you look there are people with their hands out, people with guns in their pockets. I daren't catch anybody's eye just in case they shoot me."

"And the fix is in big-time. Corruption everywhere, you know."

The sun was bright overhead. We sat in the shade. We told Richard about our adventure, exaggerating only a little.

"D'you think they were SAS or mercenaries who rescued you?"

"Dunno, I'm more interested in why they were there."

"Chasing drug barons obviously."

"I'm not so sure. There was something about them. But the guerrilla leader seemed very interested in this tour."

"You think he might want to kidnap Otis?"

"Certainly a possibility."

"No worries—we got the best security there is—which is just as well as we're starting to get some death threats."

"The drug people?"

"Probably but also from people who don't like the remarks Otis made at the press conference about their beloved queen of salsa." He looked at his watch. "What you two doing this evening—why don't I take you both to dinner?"

Five large vodka and tonics later neither were in condition to go anywhere. It wasn't the amount of booze—that amount was usually merely the beginning for both of them—it was the altitude. I was feeling very superior and smug as they reeled back to the hotel and went to their rooms, until I caught sight of myself in the mirror. My face was bright scarlet.

I waited until after dark before I left the hotel.

"High altitude, thin air, sun more powerful even in shade," the concierge said succinctly as he opened the hotel door for me.

"Thanks, pal."

I went down to a salsa club that the barman had been

recommended to me and who should be on the dance floor, large as life and twice as boisterous, but Otis. So much for altitude sickness, though I must say his drunk seemed to have gone. When he saw me watching him he looked right through me—but then a lot of people do that.

I was admiring his moves. Salsa and meringue aren't easy dances since your hips, feet, and knees are all moving at the same time but to different rhythms. For all his bulk Otis was a real snake-hips.

I'm really into South American music—the jazz mostly. Got into it with a Brazilian woman I used to hang out with in lots of Latin American joints in London. I kind of hankered for her physically but she was one of many women in history—my history—who liked me *but not like that.* They took *Mastermind* off television before I could make "Girls Who Like Me *but not like that*" my special subject.

So I ignored the woman further along the bar who was giving me little smiles and concentrated on the music—the main reason I agreed to come to Colombia with Bridget. I had a whole pile of CD from Discos Fuentes, Colombia's oldest record label.

Otis left the floor and went into the back bar with his dance partner, a pretty young woman who I was pretty sure wasn't Conchita. More salsa came on.

"You wanna dance this weeth me?"

It was the woman who had been eying me up at the bar. She was tall and statuesque with long black hair tied in a plait down her back and large brown eyes. She was tapping her foot and looking at me coquettishly.

I looked at the ferocious swirl of bodies, fast foot shuffling and heel stamping going on all around me.

"I don't think it's exactly me," I said.

"Sure eet is," she said, taking my hand and leading me onto the dance floor.

There's something very sensual about salsa—it's almost impossible not to look sexy dancing it. Almost impossible. It's my long legs and arms you see. Dancing to British music I usually look like a drunken spider. Dancing this stuff if my hips had the rhythm the rest of my body didn't. It didn't help that I'm so supple from the yoga—it just made me rubber-legged.

I laughed good-naturedly as the woman laughed at me—I'm used to it, unhappily. At the end of the dance she took me back to the bar. I was just about to offer her a drink when I saw her smile nervously at someone behind me. I looked round.

A tall, slim man in an expensive suit was standing there.

"Hey, *uomo rosso* you dance with my girlfriend," he said.

"No, thank you, I already have a dance partner."

"You dance with my girlfriend," he said more fiercely and I realized he was referring to the woman I'd been partnering in the salsa.

Hmmm. I could see where this was headed. Did I imagine the hush falling over the room?

I could either fight or run. Aside from the fact I can't fight, I was working on the assumption that every man in Bogota was linked somehow to a drug cartel, that he was armed and very dangerous, that he was a callous killer.

How to get out of this whilst maintaining my dignity—or, more to the point, my life? I wasn't sure my usual tactic—grovelling and pleading—would work here. In this country the bad guys cut off your hands and feet then beat you up for not getting out of their sight quickly enough.

I glanced quickly down at my big feet—part of the problem with my dancing perhaps. Tony Hancock had once referred to his as anarchists of the body since he didn't seem to have control over them—but this wasn't perhaps the time to dwell on that.

"Hi man, need a hand here," a familiar voice said from somewhere alongside me. It was Ralph.

# SEVEN

Seldom have I been happier to see an almost total stranger. The South American cupped his balls unconsciously and looked belligerently at the big yank. Ralph, standing easy, returned his gaze then said something in Spanish. The other guy said something back.

They talked for about five minutes, both making gestures at me, the South American's hand straying down to his crotch to make regular adjustments. Finally the guy shrugged and walked away. The woman meekly followed.

"What did you say to him?" I said.

"Told him I was your nurse. That you had a mental age of eight."

"That was pushing it wasn't it? He fell for that?"

"He thought more like five. Now where the fuck has Otis got to? Jesus it is like looking after a bunch of children."

I left whilst Ralph went over and removed Otis from the attentions of three or four amorous women of a certain age and a certain profession. I half walked, half ran back to the hotel. Bogota made me very nervous.

When I woke up in the morning my red face wasn't much better. It looked very angry. I went along the corridor to Bridget's room. I saw a familiar figure turning the corner at the far end of the corridor.

I knocked. A moment later Bridget, in her dressing gown, opened the door wide.

"What have you forgot—oh it's you."

"Did I just see Richard?" I said, walking past her into the room.

"I don't know—did you?" She gestured at my face. "Who's doing the face painting?"

"I thought you said he wasn't your type?"

"I did, didn't I?"

"You two have had sex?" I said, surprised that I felt odd about it.

"We wheezed a little together yeah. More for the companionship than anything." She dropped into a chair by the window. "You have a problem with that?"

"No, no," I said. suddenly embarrassed. Flustered I grabbed a brochure from the coffee table. It was in English and Spanish. I looked at it for a moment then at Bridget.

"Why've you got a brochure for a plastic surgery clinic?"

"Just something I picked up," she said airily. Too airily.

"Bridget?" She shuffled in her seat. It was her turn to be embarrassed.

"You get these everywhere," she said. "This is the country of drive-in plastic surgery. Way ahead on laser treatment for short-sightedness. They're nuts for it."

"Presumably got the expertise giving Nazi war criminals new identities at the end of the Second World War. They probably have templates. I'd like a Mengele, please, without the ears."

I put the brochure down.

"You're really considering plastic surgery?" I said. She shifted in her seat again. "Bloody hell, Bridget you're a bit young for that—you're only thirty-four aren't you?"

"Give or take," Bridget said.

"But what could you want doing?"

"Well, nothing really, but I hate to miss a bargain."

"Hang on—is this why you wanted to come to Colombia in the first place?"

"No, of course not, I just thought while I was here—and anyway I haven't made my mind up."

I had a sudden insight—they happen to me sometimes—based on her essentially devious nature.

"You never were going to Cartagena were you? You were checking in somewhere incognito to have some stuff done."

"So?" she said defensively.

"But Bridget, you're beautiful!"

"You should see my thighs. And look at this sagging jawline. And you should see my eyes without make-up. Not to mention the thread veins."

"Exercise. More sleep. Less booze."

"Exercise? I suppose you want me to do your yoga do you? Don't forget I've seen what you look like when you're doing it."

I do this remarkable yoga—*astanga vinyasa*—that is very energetic, very sweaty. I get so hot I usually end up looking like a boiled sweet.

Bridget had an aversion to exercise and was scathing about those who did it.

"Anyway, I haven't done it. I backed out and came down the Amazon with you—and look where that got me."

"So you're not going to have it done now?"

"Don't think so."

"You're coming on the tour?"

"What's the schedule?"

"There's a bit more time than on your usual rock tour. A couple of days in Bogota, couple in Lima, Cusco, then Macchu Picchu."

"Think I'll hang out in Bogota a bit—maybe join you in Cusco."

"You are going to do it then?"

"Maybe," Bridget said awkwardly.

She flushed a little.

"I seem to be attracting younger men and well they like you to be in shape."

"Richard's not fussy—he'll have any old boiler," I said without thinking.

My ear was still ringing when I left Bridget. Richard had set it up for me to interview Otis over lunch. But when I got to the bar there was nobody there but Otis's girlfriend Conchita sitting with three other striking Latin American women.

Bob Dylan was leaning over Conchita, taking a lingering look down her admittedly very exposed cleavage. At least it was a guy who looked just like Bob Dylan circa *Highway 61 Revisited*—long, wavy hair combed straight back, shades, the same hollow-cheeks.

When I got closer I realized this guy was a good twenty five years older than Dylan would have been back then. However, I quickly realized the Dylan look was deliberate.

"So," he was saying. "Little lady looks like she's stuck inside of Mobile with the Memphis Blues again."

Conchita looked up at him. I was thinking that's just what this tour needs—a Dylan nut. He started to sing—badly.

"She makes love just like a woman but she breaks just like a little girl—" he suddenly resumed his speaking voice—"you see it right there, man does that dude know the innermost places of all our beings or what?"

His accent was one of those phony mid–Atlantic ones British DJs used to favor before Cockney conquered all. I realized who he was—Benny, Otis's long ago bass player now playing percussion with the Fertile Lands. Since I knew he came from Stoke on Trent his drawl lacked a certain authenticity.

"What you know about the way I make love?" Conchita hissed at him.

"He's quoting," I said.

"All I'm saying is you look like the sad-eyed lady of the lowlands to me. I was you I wouldn't put up with no shit from that Otis—I mean what is this—fourth time around?"

"Is *Blonde on Blonde* the only album you know?" I said.

Perry grinned—he obviously had fun doing this.

"Just pledging my time to the little lady, though I know ma'am that most likely you'll go your way, I'll go mine."

"You darn tootin' there, meester," Conchita said.

"I'm just letting you know you got a tight connection to my heart," he said, winking at me. Okay, so he did know other albums.

"Yeah?" said Conchita, a wicked smile on her face. She stuck a finger in the air, its long purple nail some half an inch long.

"See this? Swivel on it why doncha?"

Benny straightened and started to walk away.

"Mighty kind offer, mighty kind," he said. "But I think I'll pass on that just now."

I looked down at Conchita. I was willing to give odds on her in a ruckus with Bridget. I introduced myself.

"Hi Nick, Otis is running a little late. These are my friends—a group of Latin American artists all exploring the traditional association of Latin America with the female body."

"Is there a traditional association?" I said.

"Sure thing—what do Westerners think of when they think of South America—half naked girls dancing in the carnival."

Personally I thought of llamas but I didn't want to be misunderstood so I said nothing.

"Beauty contests," Conchita went on. "We take beauty contests so seriously wars have been fought about them."

I nodded, thinking about Bridget and her plastic surgery.

"This is Cesar," Conchita said to me indicating a buxom woman in a mannish trouser suit. "She does a performance in which she invites the audience to eat a life-size body made of jelly. Stuffed with tropical fruit, presented on an operating table. Invited to eat your favorite parts until figure has disappeared."

"How ... innovative."

"You should try my wobbly bits," she said, giving me an up-from-under look.

"Indeed." I smiled. "And what do you do?" I said to the next one, sounding alarmingly like Prince Charles trying to be at one with his people.

"I have a three-day performance in which I go through the everyday cycle of waking, eating, and watching TV until it becomes a poetic ritual. I'm a living relic, creating an installation from the trace of my presence."

"I'm sure you are."

The final one was Argentinian. Her performance consisted of filling a room with maize as a repayment of the Argentinian foreign debt to Margaret Thatcher. You see why I prefer movies?

They left shortly after.

"Otis is sleeping off his hangover. Why don't we start lunch and he can join us when he gets up?"

Conchita led the way out onto the terrace. She was a beautiful woman and all the waiters were agog to see her. They gave us a table for three. When we were settled and had ordered our meals, I said:

"Otis caused quite a lot of controversy with his remarks about you yesterday. How did you feel about him talking about you like that?"

"He is a little boy—he likes to shock. I was not insulted. It was the men in my country who would like to be the ones in my bed—they were the ones who were insulted because they are jealous."

"Interesting point of view," I said, bemused by her logic.

The waiter came. She ordered in rapid Spanish.

"What was that you ordered?"

"Bull's testicles."

There was silence that I felt the need to fill.

"So you tried to cut off his, er ..."

"His what—his pizzle?" She waved the knife in her hand absently in the air. "Sure—I grew up on a farm. By the age of twelve I know how to turn a stud stallion into a gelding."

"Fancy," I said, squeezing my thighs together.

"What are you doin', woman?" a voice said.

I looked up. Otis loomed over me, an angry expression on his face. In his anger he had reverted to his Scottish accent. His face was flushed and his eyes were bulging and bloodshot. I couldn't help also noticing that he had shoulders like a bull and forearms like ham.

She bridled at his tone.

"Having lunch, what it look like?"

"Who's he?" he said gesturing with his thumb without looking at me.

"Er—" I said, not because I didn't know who I was but because I was surprised by his hostility. Conchita's eyes flashed.

"My lover, of course, we're having a romantic meal together."

"Er—" (That was me again.)

"So I can fuckin' see," he said, loud enough for people at the other tables to turn and look our way.

"Go fuck yourself why doncha?" Conchita piped up helpfully. "I have lunch with whoever I wan. You sleep all day, thass my problem?"

He looked at me now but snarled at her.

"Shut it, woman."

I was sure he was going to hit me and I was trying to figure out how to get up from the table before he did so. Not to fight him, to defend myself. Or preferably to run like hell.

"It's not how it seems—" I started to say.

He held the palm of his hand up in front of my face in a stop right there gesture. His eyes bulged.

"And you shut it too, you long streak of piss."

I wanted to say I wasn't accustomed to being talked to like that. Sadly, it's not true. I'm always being talked to like that—the world seems to be full of belligerent men, most of whom take a dislike to me.

Otis pulled the third chair out and sat down heavily. I clutched my dessert spoon more tightly. Well, no, I'd never heard of anyone successfully defending themselves from an angry gorilla with a piece of cutlery but I had few options.

His big red hands, with their heavy scarring on the knuckles, were bunched into fists.

I was temporarily distracted by wondering how he could play such delicate guitar—he often finger-picked in the classical way without using a plectrum—with such thick fingers. Only temporarily though.

"I was supposed to be having lunch with you but you didn't show so Conchita offered to keep me company until you did show."

"Yeah, Conchita would. She likes keeping company with men—the more the merrier."

It depressed me no end to discover that this guy who's music I loved was turning out to be such a pig. I hated his shitty attitude to women.

And sometimes you've just got to make a stand against it. I looked at the way his muscles were bunched in his shoulders and biceps, at the rage in his face. Of course, my stand didn't have to be now.

Unfortunately my mouth often tends to work independently of my brain.

"You're an objectionable excuse for a man aren't you, you bullying fuck."

I heard the words a split second before I realized they had issued from my mouth. I didn't catch his reply. But then the ringing in my ears, the clatter of my chair as it fell over backwards, and the crockery cascade off the table as I dragged the tablecloth with me drowned everything else out.

I'd seen the Bogota national stadium on my way in from the airport. It gave me the chills because I associated sports stadia in South America with human rights violations, useful for herding together political dissidents and opponents of repressive regimes.

The Bogota stadium was the place where in some future civil upheaval the Colombian opposition would be sequestered, tortured, then slaughtered.

I looked across at Otis and Conchita sitting side by side in the back seat of the limo. All friends again.

Otis hadn't knocked me out but he had sent me flying. When I struggled to my feet—still clutching my spoon, one part of my brain was amused to observe—Ralph had already appeared from nowhere and was standing over me.

I looked beyond him to where Otis was still sitting at the table, a mirthless grin on his face.

I got to my feet, shedding shards of crockery, and made a move towards him. Ralph blocked my way. My ears were ringing and the right side of my face felt both numb and hot. I made to go past Ralph.

"Let me at him," I growled, "I'll fucking kill him."

Ralph held me back—thank God. I mean I had to make a show of anger but I knew Otis could do me serious damage if I tried anything. So I said a couple of other tough guy things, struggled—but not too much—to get out of Ralph's grip.

When he decided my honor had been salved Ralph raised
an eyebrow at me and let me go. This guy knew me too well.
I looked around. Waiters were hovering. The few other diners
in the restaurant at that time of day were watching these mad
foreigners with interest. Conchita merely sipped her drink,
watching me through narrowed eyes.

Otis's anger seemed to have dissipated when I resumed my
seat.

"A little slap across the face—didn't take much, did it, pal?"
he commented matter of factly.

"Yeah well I don't judge a man by how fast he is with his
fists."

"Oh yeah?" He leered. "How do you judge him then?" He
grabbed his tackle. "By the size of his johnson?"

"You better hope not, Otis, or you in big trouble," Conchita
said.

Otis flashed a look at her but a moment later burst out
laughing.

Just then Richard arrived and calmed everybody down. He
got Otis to apologize to me, which he did in a very winning way
and then invited me to travel with Otis and Conchita out to the
national stadium for the sound-check.

Which is where I was headed now.

I was sitting in one of the bucket seats facing back in the
limo. The other was occupied by Otis's manager, Horace.

I was quite enjoying the ride. I'd never been in a stretch
limo before and certainly not one that was bomb proof. Ralph
was sitting up front with a machine pistol in his lap. The driver
was also armed.

I've got to confess I didn't take to the manager. Cockney
slick, with that hard talking wise-ass style of delivery patented by
the yob intellectuals who had taken over TV in recent years.

He wanted desperately to be hip but he just hadn't got it. He wore a sharp black suit that looked like he'd been poured into it and forgotten to say when. I also saw to my horror that he wore socks with cartoon characters on them. I was shocked to think people still did that.

It's long been my contention that there should be separate parts of restaurants for any of the following: cartoon socks, women wearing long chiffon scarves or patterned tights or white boots or court shoes with either jeans or cords; men wearing their weekday striped shirts open-necked at the weekend with jeans and polished black shoes. In addition, people with loud shirts would be forced to sit and let their clothes shout at each other.

Don't even get me started on leather trousers.

Worse than the cartoon socks was the fact that Otis's manager had a laugh that screamed nutter. It was low but it went on for too long and it erupted in the wrong places. He clearly had no sense of humor. He was like an alien. To blend in he knew he should be laughing, that laughing was good but he laughed in the wrong places because he didn't know what was funny.

My impression of him must have shown on my face. When I looked Otis was giving me a sardonic look. I didn't know where else to look, actually, because I was trying not to look at Conchita. She was packed into a low cut very short dress and every time she moved I broke into a sweat.

And I couldn't help noticing that the jeep with the other guards bringing up the rear was about an inch from our rear bumper. Given we were going at about fifty miles an hour on a crowded road, this gave me pause for thought. Otis seemed to read my mind.

"I love the fucking driving in this city—oh man," he said shaking his head. I frowned. "We've gone through three red lights in a row."

"That's the way it works here," Horace said, without looking up from the sheaf of papers he was examining. I shuffled the papers I had in a folder on my lap in what I hoped was an important way.

"You're a potential target—as a hostage or worse—so the drivers don't stop at red lights, don't stop at road junctions since that's where terrorists mostly strike. See the motorcyclist up ahead?"

I craned in my seat and beyond the advance car, packed with guys with guns, could see a motorcyclist weaving through traffic. I nodded.

"He's our point guy—he goes ahead stops other traffic."

"How?" I said.

"Rides out in front of it, blows his whistle, and sticks up his hand."

"And does that work?" I asked, as we all heard the screech of tires, blare of horns, and the terrible sound of metal crunching into metal. Our car broke abruptly and he and I were pressed back into our seats. I saw the jeep behind us loom even closer in the back window, felt the jolt, and heard more metal grind as the jeep went into our rear.

"Most of the time," I heard Ralph growl from his seat in the front.

# EIGHT

None of us was hurt much, though my eye watered for the next half hour or so. When the car braked Otis and Conchita had been thrown forward against their seat belts. For Conchita this meant putting even more strain on a dress that was clearly unequal to the task of constraining her large breasts. The manager and I were pressed deep into our seats.

When the jeep then jolted our car forward it jolted Otis and Conchita, too. Conchita's back was arched and the jolt made it seem as if she were playing some game where you had to toss your breasts without using your hands. Her breasts bounced—the left one right out of the dress.

I just had time to marvel at her engorged nipple when the reverse force took effect on my body. I wasn't wearing a seat belt. My papers shot off my lap onto the floor—I was aware of the manager's doing the same—and I toppled forward as Conchita hung suspended between coming forward and falling back.

Her nipple caught me right in the eye. Better than a poke with a sharp stick you might think and that was my first thought, but then I came into contact with the beautiful breast behind the nipple. Bad enough that her nipple had almost taken my eye out but the surgically enhanced breast was unyielding in the extreme.

I scrabbled away from her as rapidly as I could, uncomfortably aware that as I sprawled across her, her skirt had ridden right up around her hips and I was virtually mounting her.

Otis pushed me back into my seat.

"Got an eyeful did you?" he said, with an expression on his face that I wasn't sure meant he was joking.

"Sorry," I mumbled as the manager came back out of his seat again, scrabbling for his papers. I felt I had to do the same, if only so he wouldn't see mine was some poetry I'd been fiddling with.

There I've said it. I write poetry. Oh I may not be a sensitive police commander knocking off the odd melancholy sonnet in between solving crimes but I've had my moments. Well, moment.

When I was a student, a poem of mine about King Arthur and Guinevere—I know, I know, I'm blushing more than you're cringing, believe me—was published in the university literary magazine.

That wasn't the thrill. I've always had a pretty utilitarian view of writing. The thrill was the fact that the poem's publication led to my seduction by a young pre-Raphaelite type who was quite taken by my sensitivity.

It ended in tears—when haven't my affairs?—but then she did identify rather strongly in the Arthurian story cycle with Eleanor, a.k.a. the droopy woman who killed herself for love of Lancelot.

I was no Lancelot—no corny jokes about Lance alittle here, thank you—and she was certainly no droopy woman. I bought her a dress—Laura Ashley, natch—and she tore it in half with her teeth because she didn't like the pattern. Intense? I should say so.

I swept my papers up and stuffed them into my red file. The manager tidied the rest and bunged them in his briefcase before shooting out of the car door.

I thought he was going to see how the motorcyclist was,

and indeed he did go over to him. The boot had sprung open and whilst the bodyguards from the jeep stood round the car in loose formation, guns trained outwards, the motorcyclist could have been bribed or threatened to fall there to prepare us for an ambush, the driver tried to close the lid.

It kept springing up again. The manager came back over with the very hound-dog looking motorcyclist, who was limping and had blood on him, though from where I wasn't sure. A rapid conversation in Spanish ensued, then the motorcyclist, looking even more hound-dog, climbed into the boot. The driver shut the boot on him.

"You've put him in the boot?" I said when Horace returned.

"He was shaky, he needed to lie down so I thought he could do it there and hold the lid closed at the same time."

And that's what he did. For the rest of the journey through Bogota's pot-holed streets, I was conscious of these fingers curled round the lip of the boot door holding it down.

The national stadium was in a busy part of town. The fleet of cars was given immediate access. We swept in and parked round the back of the stadium. The guards—we had about a dozen with us and a further couple of dozen dotted round the stadium—were on full alert. They still weren't certain if the motorcyclist's accident had been a set-up.

The stage had been set up at one end of the immense stadium; it had seating for a couple of hundred thousand easily. Banks of speakers twenty feet high towered over the stage at either end. There was an inflatable bouncy castle round the back—it's the kind of thing rock musicians, all children at heart, like to play on, for a few moments at least. Otis went on stage and hugged the two or three people who were up there.

The tour had brought its own crew, partly for security reasons and partly because they had with them the best in the business. These were the guys that could work forty-eight hours without a break, wire up an entire city, and still find time to score a woman in the intervals.

So people said. I must say, these guys didn't look too prepossessing. The usual overweight guys with grey pigtails, builders' cleavages on full display. They had that cliquish distance of people who feel not only are they hip, they are also part of an elite.

In short, they ignored me. I didn't mind. I got myself a seat in the bleachers on the side of the stage and watched what was going on. The paranoid part of me was on the lookout for Porras and his guerrillas but the rational part of me said that was nonsense.

Sometimes of course being paranoid is the only rational way to be. Way down at the end of the field I saw a jeep turn in and start slowly towards the stage some 500 yards away. As it picked up speed with a throaty roar of its engine one or two other people glanced over at it.

There was no way to be certain there was anything peculiar about this jeep. Until, that is, the driver leapt out when it was a hundred yards away, did a roll away from the car, and started running back the way he had come, towards a black speck that quickly became a scooter. It reached the running man and he got on the pillion. A getaway on a scooter? *The Italian Job* come back, all is forgiven.

The jeep was heading straight for the stage. A couple of security guards drew their weapons and moved towards it. Otis suddenly appeared at the back of the stage, walking slowly upstage, big headphones on, focused on tuning his guitar. The guards hadn't seen him. As far as they knew he was backstage.

A couple of guards took potshots at the jeep but another shouted for them to desist, presumably because they didn't want any explosives on board to be detonated. He spoke rapidly into his radio mike.

When the jeep was within fifty yards of the stage the paralysis of the guards suddenly broke. They started to hustle everyone out of the way. At this point Otis's limo came round the side of the stage and set out to head off the jeep.

The jeep was going at about twenty mph, the speeding limo about fifty. The driver approached at an angle, slowed his speed to about twenty-five mph then rammed the front left side of the jeep. The limo's boot popped open.

The height was wrong. The jeep tilted but kept going straight as an arrow. People scattered. I was about to do the same when I saw a figure emerge from inside the boot and look around in total bewilderment. The motorcyclist.

Oops. He saw the jeep and, all credit to the man, grasped the situation quickly. The limo was riding alongside the jeep, trying to nudge it off to the side. The jeep didn't want to be nudged.

I had to look away when the motorcyclist reached across and grabbed the jeep door on the passenger side. His problem was the limo driver didn't know he was there so when he suddenly accelerated the motorcyclist had two options—he could stay with the jeep or with the limo.

There was a third option—he could have his arms wrenched from his sockets. Brave, foolhardy, or just plain stupid, he opted to go with the jeep, the velocity pulling him out of the boot and leaving him hanging, knees crouched to his chest off the door of the jeep.

I didn't see what happened next because when I looked away I spotted Otis, still twiddling with his guitar strings quite oblivious to what was going on around him, shielded from public view by the towering speakers.

I waved my arms at him but he didn't see me. I looked back at the jeep. The motorcyclist was grappling with the door. The limo meanwhile was doing a big loop to pull across in front of it. It was about twenty yards from the stage.

Saying a quick prayer to the God of idiots I ran across the stage and hurled myself at Otis.

I was never a rugby player at school, hated all that macho stuff. If I'd thought about how to take him down I probably wouldn't have done it. If he'd been wearing the guitar strapped to his body I definitely wouldn't have done it.

But he had laid the guitar down to tune it, using one of those computerized gizmos. I hit him around the waist from the side. He'd half seen me and had started to pull off the headphones before I hit him. We both went off the back of the stage.

The drop was vertiginous but coming almost immediately back up was dizzying. We'd landed on the bouncy castle.

On the second bounce I let go of him so he could bounce to his own rhythm whilst I tensed for the explosion on-stage.

It came in my head instead. Otis bounced towards me and took a lazy swing at my head with a balled fist. I moved my head but the bounce was against me and he caught me on the jaw. I went down—and presumably back up again though I had no way of knowing since he'd knocked me out.


I don't react well to violence. I certainly don't react to somebody punching me in the face. Maybe I've got an especially sensitive brain but having it bang around inside my skull with the impact of a blow does me no good at all.

I woke up, looked up, threw up.

Not because Otis was looming over me—I was getting used to that—but because that's the kind of guy I am. To give him his due he didn't act all disgusted as my projectile vomit went all over his feet. Didn't even look down. That's what I call a man. Or a drunk.

For I couldn't help noticing as he leaned towards me that he gave off an overpowering smell of booze. His eyes were watery and unfocused again.

"Sorry pal, thought you were being a dickhead," he said. "But it looks like you were trying to protect me, which is more than all these other tossers were doing."

I sat up slowly. My head was thudding and there was a sudden shooting pain in my eyes. For a moment I was reminded of sex—but I've been told before I do it wrong.

"Did the bomb go off?" I mumbled.

Ralph the security guy's head came into view.

"Nothing on board. Just a hoax. Or a warning."

"D'you get the guys?"

"Perps walked," Ralph said.

"Don't you love that?" Otis said, grinning madly. "I love that fucking laconic way of talking."

He lowered his voice and pushed his chin into his neck. "Perps walked. The fucking concision of it. That's why I'm an honorary—"

"Honorary what?" Ralph said sharply, clearly suspecting some racist remark was in the offing.

"Yank. I just love that bare bones language. Don't always understand it but I love it."

"It's certainly terse," I said.

"Terse, good word," Otis agreed. "Laconic now, there's an odd word—sounds like somebody is really relaxed, affable, chatty—doesn't mean any of that, of course, means the same as terse."

Fine time to have a discussion about the meaning of words. Ralph was still deciding whether to be hostile or not. I could see his point.

I touched my jaw, flexed it gingerly. Nothing seemed to be damaged.

"Who were those guys?" Otis said, helping me to my feet.

"Couple of *sicano*," Ralph said. Otis raised an eyebrow.

"Punks, hired assassins. Usually does it from a scooter. It's the kind of teenage hoodlum the drug barons hire. These are kids with death in their eyes. Don't expect to live long. All they care about is dressing well and driving a good scooter. They're hired to *hacer un trabajo*—to do a job, a kill."

I nodded. Ralph raised himself to his impressively full height.

"What you've got to recognize is that the drug trade fills a vacuum in Colombia. For centuries about thirty families have owned pretty much all of Colombia. Carved it up between them a couple of hundred years ago. Over the centuries they've just used it as a resource, exploiting the country and the people, banking the profits.

"So for a long time most people have been little more than slaves, scraping a living. The real economy is in terrible shape. Then the drugs come along and suddenly there's another economy, another way to make money.

"The towns and cities are still filled with no-hopers but at least if they go to work for the drug barons they can earn some money. But only for a while, because the work they do isn't conducive to a long life. These guys are suicide killers, human bombs. All they care about are designer clothes, a scooter, and guns. They want to look good to their friends, in the same line of business, and they're full of such macho bullshit that the only way they know to impress is to be foolhardy.

"So yeah they die young. Usually around fifteen when they get hired, sixteen or seventeen when they die. One of them comes for you you'd best hide because he don't give a shit."

"So what was this—a warning from the drug barons?"

"A warning sure enough to show what could have happened if they'd wanted to. But as for who they is—could be the barons, could be the right wing death squads—they're pretty pissed at us coming down here poking our noses in their affairs."

"What about guerrillas?"

"Doesn't look like guerrilla stuff—there's no percentage

in this for them."

"I was kidnapped by a guerrilla leader called Ferdinand Porras. He has a possible motive."

"Porras is a big fish but I don't know why he would be interested," Ralph said.

"He has a grudge against Otis."

Otis looked surprised. Befuddled actually.

"Ferdinand Porras? Don't know the guy."

"Not back in London?"

Otis scratched his head.

"Knew a Freddy Porras once, a sax player. Ben Webster going on David Sanborn. Last time I saw him was in a squat in Ladbroke Grove. A lifetime ago."

"That's the one," I said. "Small matter of stealing his wife."

"Freddy Porras? Freddy Porras is a guerrilla leader? You're shitting me! I mean he played killer saxophone but that's still quite a career leap."

"Trust me, it's him," I said, describing the man I'd seen in the Amazon. Otis believed me—first person ever.

"Always wondered what happened to him—he just dropped out of sight. Guess you can never tell which way a jazzer is going to leap."

"Did you steal his wife?"

"What the hell was her name now? Lindy? Lindsay? Hell no. I maybe borrowed her for a little, just like everybody else did. She wasn't exactly discriminating."

Otis looked at me a little blearily.

"Freddy told you that?" I nodded. "Don't suppose he told you he wasn't exactly a saint himself. Fucked anything with a heartbeat. Good-looking guy—chicks came on to him all the time. But see, your typical Latino, it's okay for him to do that but not for his wife to fool around."

"Sound familiar to you?" I said.

I thought for a moment he was going to hit me again. Instead he looked sheepish and scratched his head.

"I reckon," he said. He looked around. "Ralph, I'm going to leave security to you. Where's my band—we've got rehearsals to do. Think you'd better have a lie-down, Mick, you're looking a bit peaky."

"Nick."

"Sure. Ralph here will get someone to take you back to the hotel."

Ralph took me himself. I couldn't figure the guy—his perpetual bad humor—but he was a straight talker and I valued that.

"We've had a few death threats directed at Otis."

"Anonymous of course."

"Not always. An extreme right wing death squad has sent a threat in. The squad is the usual mix of off-duty policemen, militia, and military who've been hiring themselves out to the shopkeepers to kill the street-kids who are bad for business. Not too happy about us interfering, as they see it, with their internal politics. Half a dozen threats because of the remarks he made about Conchita—Otis has a worrisome attitude to women. Then one really weird one, which may well just be a fan note, arrived as I was leaving the hotel."

"May I see it?"

"Sure," Ralph said, digging in his pocket and handing it over.

The message was printed—very carefully—on hotel stationary, available in the lobby of our hotel. I recognized it immediately. It was a quote from the lyrics of one of Otis's early songs.

I hate song lyrics printed out as if they were holy texts, especially as 99 percent of them don't scan, read tritely—I always cringe when I hear that clunky line from John Lennon's Imagine "And no religion, too." Even my dad, who of course thought Lennon was God used to scream at the record player:

"*Either*—no religion *either*."

The worrying thing is that people found this so moving—must have really pissed off true poets, who marry rhyme with emotions so beautifully, that people are moved by something so clunky.

Still at least this guy kept the excerpt brief and to the point.

"*Fond as equals.* Killed by desire."

Well, you had to read it in context. Ripped out of context it wasn't very poetic but it could be a death threat. Maybe.

"What's the next one?"

"You speak Spanish?"

I shook my head.

"Okay then, loosely translates as 'You're fucking dead.'"

"Not much ambiguity about that."

"Not so much as a hint. Goes on to say how they're gonna cut off his johnson and stuff it down his throat."

"The cheaper the punk, the gaudier the patter," I said, surprising myself remembering the lines from *The Maltese Falcon*. Then I realized why—Colombia was being run by gangsters.

"In this country that's the least people do to other people. It actually shows a lack of imagination—most villains do far worse.

Back in my hotel room I lay on the bed and closed my eyes. I thought I'd settle my pounding head by going into the resting pose, relaxing every limb and breathing deeply.

Usually I could do this no problem. I recommend it for those unable to sleep at night. But the fact that the popular name for the position is the corpse posture—well let's just say it had resonances in Colombia that were too close for comfort.

I swung my feet off the bed and walked over to my case. I was feeling moon-in-June-ish.

I'd started writing poetry again on the advice of my therapist. There I've said it. Therapist, therapist, therapist. I'd started going just after I'd met up with an old girlfriend of my dad's. It was my therapist who suggested I go back to writing poetry to help express my long dormant feelings.

"Long dormant feelings about what?" I said.

"Your hatred of your father and your desire for your mother."

"Steady on," I said. I mean I knew she was a strict Freudian but my mother had died when I was three, for goodness sake.

My dad died when I was eighteen and in many ways it was a relief, though I suspected I'd lived my life ever since in a kind of symbiotic relationship with him.

And his various addictions. Thank God he was too much of a hippy to try glue-sniffing or my Aerofix kits of balsa-wood planes would never have been completed.

I remember Bridget coming to my flat in Shepherds Bush soon after I'd started the therapy. "What the fuck are these?" she said, looking at the ceiling. She lazily reached out her hand and flicked with her fingernail.

"Careful Bridget," I said, rushing over to cup my hands around the plane—a Messerschmidt if you want to get technical—that was now swinging wildly on the length of string by which it was suspended from the ceiling. A drawing pin held it in place.

"Well?" she said.

"What?"

"What the fuck are these?

"Planes."

"I thought mobiles were meant to chime or something."

"These aren't mobiles." I blushed.

"If it's not a mobile what are they doing? Why are they each on a different length of string?"

"Aesthetics," I said vaguely.

Bridget snorted.

"You wouldn't know an aesthetic if it bit you on the bum."

"I made them when I was a kid. They're having a dog-fight."

I didn't give her bellow of laughter the dignity of a response. I was rather proud of my dogfight. The Spitfires coming out of the sun—that was a lamp on the mantelpiece—to attack the Messerschmidts with a few other odds and sods that didn't quite fit, like a MG11. It had taken me ages to do.

Putting them up as a kind of homage to my childhood was my therapist's idea. It's what I would have liked to do when I was a kid but a) I didn't have the patience and b) it wouldn't have lasted five minutes because my dad would have got tangled in it the minute he walked in drunk from the pub.

I could picture him waking up the next morning in a chair he slept in if he passed out before he hit the bedroom, a turban of broken planes round his forehead.

But I digress. The therapy—well, it was just good to talk to somebody who would listen. At least I assume she was listening. She might have been asleep for all I knew—it's happened before. Sure, I could have said the same things to my best friend, except Bridget is my best friend and I can't even get a word in edgeways with her.

The only thing my therapist said to me was, "We all have an inner child, Nick, but for some people it's not quite so inner."

Bridget's laughter went on for quite a long time then. Finally I said: "Well, haven't you got anything of your childhood in your place. I bet you have cuddly toys."

Bridget curled her lip, making her look like Cliff in *Espresso Bongo*, without the quiff and obviously, the bongos.

I wandered over to the window and when she wasn't looking tucked my teddy more firmly behind the pillow on my rolled-up futon.

That was the problem with therapy. I'd read a lot about it

before I went into it and I was very sceptical—as far as I was concerned people who went into therapy needed *their* heads examined.

I was always reminded of that Groucho Marx joke: "You're on the edge of a nervous breakdown. Why don't you hurry up and pull yourself apart."

I knew my therapist wasn't perhaps all she was cracked up to be. If you'll excuse the expression.

Anyway, when I did a little research—I am a journalist after all, even though clearly one who is slow off the mark—I discovered you don't need to be qualified to be a therapist. Anyone can set themselves up as one.

When I asked her about her qualifications she admitted under my experienced questioning that she didn't have any. Well, actually she told me to fuck off but eventually admitted it. She'd been a PE instructor and had hurt her knee, so needed some alternative employment, especially as her husband had just left her.

She had also been a company wife—a lifetime of having to listen to her husband whining at home and other men mouthing off at do's, and she figured she may as well get paid for it.

I think her subtext was that if she could screw up a few men up in the process all the better.

The other giveaway was that when I started opening my heart to her she gave an impatient sigh and said, "For God's sake don't whine." I'm sure I also heard her say "What a wimp," under her breath.

"But I'm paying you to let me whine," I said. "Nobody will listen to me voluntarily."

I realized later she was cribbing from some book, reading the next chapter and keeping just far enough ahead of me so that she seemed wise. Not that she said much. That was the beauty of being a strict Freudian. They never say anything.

You can't even see them—you lie on the couch and they sit out of sight behind you. I could hear the scratching of her pen so I know she was there—though once I'm sure I heard a little snort, one of those beginnings of a snore—but for all I knew she could have been doing a crossword.

I stopped going to her, took down the dogfight but carried on with the poetry. To be honest, under the impress of the rock tour I was trying to write songs.

I got my folder out of my case. All my papers were scrambled because of the jolt in the car.

I lay on the bed again, sorting them with the help of a drink from the mini-bar. Near the bottom of the pile I came upon a few unfamiliar sheets of paper. I looked at them puzzled then realized they must have been some of Horace's papers that had somehow got mixed up with mine.

I read them, then again more closely. One in particular stood out. I didn't understand all the legal jargon but the meaning was clear.

In the event of Otis's death everything—and I mean everything—went to Horace, his manager.

# NINE

I didn't see Horace at the concert in the evening. He wasn't in the green room—actually a trapezoid tent erected backstage beside the bouncy castle. There were sofas and two long tables, one laid with plates of tapas, the other with every sort of booze imaginable.

From the side of the stage I looked out over the stadium. It looked pretty full—a sea of people who celebrated the appearance of their Latin American heroes with a fusillade of firecrackers. When the first ones went off I saw Ralph tense.

I could see that he was kitted out with the latest electronic communications technology—headphones with a tiny microphone jutting out beside his jaw—though I couldn't actually see his face.

But then I was down on hands and knees behind one of the banks of speakers. How was I to know they were firecrackers? One of the Fertile Lands—the next band up—gave me an odd look.

"Contact lens," I mouthed, feeling on the floor around me, then carefully lifting my index finger towards my eye. Considering I didn't wear contact lenses I thought my mime was pretty good.

Pity that just as my finger reached my eye the second fusillade went off. I jerked and poked myself in the same eye Conchita had poked me in earlier.

Conchita was on stage and her set was going down a treat. But then this was her home crowd. She wore a figure-hugging dress—did she have any other sort?—and danced around the stage non-stop as she sang her greatest Latin American hits, her rhythm section belting out a dense, fast rhythm.

By the time she bounced offstage drenched in sweat, her face shiny, her dress like a second skin, the entire stadium was up and dancing and the atmosphere was electric. She gave me a little wave as she passed by. I mimed applause.

The Fertile Lands shambled on stage. Since the audience were up for dancing and Fertile Lands played some hippy-dippy world music through conches, gourds, some kind of bagpipe, and various other unlikely instruments, I was waiting for the real shooting to start—this was after all the continent where wars broke out over the results of football matches.

But the audience calmed down on hearing the weird combination of Celtic, African, and South American music. They listened to the set with rapt attention.

Watching the band, I was struck by the lead singer, a slender blonde in glasses with her hair tied in a convoluted system of braids.

Benny was the oldest person in the band. I watched him as he shambled off stage at the end and walked straight to the bar. He popped the cap off a bottle of beer and glugged it down in one, his head thrown back, his bony Adam's apple bobbing to keep up with his thirst. He picked up another bottle, flicked the top off with his thumb—I was impressed to see—and looked around the room.

He watched me walk over.

"Hi," I said, "I'm Nick Madrid. I enjoyed your set."

"I'm thrilled for you." He took a swig from the bottle.

"No Dylan quotes today? What's with the Dylan lookalike anyway?"

"Everybody wants to be someone else—what's it to you?"

"I hear you used to play with Otis—must be a surprise being on the same bill as him again after—how many years is it?"

"Ten years—and the only surprise is the bugger's still alive. Thought he would have drunk himself to death by now."

"Thought or hoped?"

He gave me a sidelong look for a long moment.

"You the Scoop?"

"That I am. And you're the guy who thinks he should have a percentage of Otis's takings. Must cause a bit of tension here."

"That's business mate—let my lawyer worry about that stuff. Me, I'm into the eternal whatsit," he looked past me, "with my fellow-musicians here."

I turned as the woman with the braided blonde hair joined us. She lowered her glasses and peered over them at me.

"Beatrice, meet Scoop. Scoop, Beatrice."

"You the person who does the yoga?" Beatrice said.

The percussionist sniggered. Here we go again.

"Why?"

"Have I touched a nerve?" she said, stepping back. "Richard told me about it, that's all. It sounds very interesting. Perhaps you could show me sometime."

How I loved those six words.

Benny gave me a sardonic grin then wandered away with his bottle of beer. Beatrice smiled, waiting for me to speak.

I was curious why. She was beautiful and talented. I am, if I'm honest, a dork. I have a hard-earned rule of thumb about women, a variation on Groucho's line about a club that will have him as a member: If a woman finds me attractive there must be something wrong with her.

This isn't self-pity or self-deprecation. It's based on experience. I'm totally sexist in that I tend to go for great-looking women. But I'm not a great-looking man. I'm big and in reasonable shape—well, aside from the child-bearing hips—but that's as far as it goes.

So if a good-looking woman seems interested I'm nervous because I know there's going to be something wrong with her. Some little foible like axe-murderer. Manic depression is a popular one. Schizoid, paranoiac, and downright murderous—I've known 'em all.

But I want to be clear about this—in bed I've disappointed them equally without fear or favor. Based on what a former girlfriend had told Bridget she had once said I should wear a badge saying, "Not worth the heartache ladies."

The same old girlfriend once told an assembled dinner party: "Poor Nick, he tries so hard."

I used to warn women in advance not to expect too much—anything in fact—but could never get the timing right. Too early and they accused me of presumption, got huffy and that was the end of it. Too late and it was, well, too late.

So as I told Beatrice, at her request, about the yoga, I looked for those tell-tale signs—the flecks of foam at the mouth, the unblinking gaze, the laughing at the wrong moment.

Nothing. She took her glasses off and wiped them on a tissue a couple of times but I couldn't read much into that. This made me more nervous because of her inevitable disappointment.

I thought I'd take the opportunity to quiz her about Benny.

"How long has Benny been in your band?"

"Couple of years."

"Has he ever said anything about Otis?"

"You mean the record thing? Nothing—but then he doesn't mix with us very much. He's on salary—fixed-fee. We three others do the writing."

"Not worried he's going to try the same number with you?"

"You don't think his claim is genuine?"

"Dunno. Does he bear grudges?"

"He's quick to take offence. I think it's the drink. We've had to hush up a couple of incidents in bars. Glassed one bloke, bottled another."

"Why do you keep him in the band? Your music isn't the kind you associate with that kind of behavior."

She flashed me a smile and leaned towards me conspiratorially.

"Johnny, the leader of the group, has kind of taken to him—they're drinking buddies, I think."

"Don't you find it a bit hypocritical being on a tour against drugs on which everybody drinks so much?"

"Absolutely," she said with a grin. "This gig's great exposure for the band, though."

Otis took the stage at this point. There was some hissing, some boos. I glanced over at Ralph who was speaking quickly into his mike. There was a bang, then another and another.

More firecrackers—but perfect camouflage for anyone wanting to shoot Otis and slip away.

Although I had decided Otis was a pig and a major disappointment, I respected his bravery in going on stage knowing his life had been threatened.

As he started with his first song and another flurry of firecrackers ripped the air, I had a startling thought—maybe no one had told him about the death threats.

Otis went down a bomb, so to speak. After the initial hisses he soon won people around. He was on great form, switching between rockers and ballads, up tempo and lazily slow. He did three encores. By the time Conchita joined him, resplendent in a swirling scarlet skirt, to duet on a couple of love songs, he had clearly been forgiven—the audience went nuts, especially when the pair kissed at the end.

I looked at Beatrice.

"A bit of a triumph, I'd say."

She shrugged.

"Are you going back to the hotel?" I said.

"Band is going out for a meal. Sorry. But what about the yoga, tomorrow at Baza?"

"What's Baza?" I said, but with a swift peck on the cheek she was gone.

I shared a taxi back with Richard and a journalist from *Rolling Stone* named Perry. I arrived in time to see Ralph hustle Otis from the limo into the hotel. There was still no sign of Horace.

Richard looked at me.

"Bar?"

"Pope? Bear?"

When we were settled I said:

"Is Otis a wealthy man?"

"Done pretty well out of the last album and single. But all the money he earns goes to pay off debts he accumulated in the bad days. He makes your financial management positively statesmanlike."

"Has Horace got many other clients?"

"Not that I'm aware of—why?"

"So what money he makes is dependent on Otis?"

"Do you want to let me in on this or are you going to carry on being oblique?"

I looked around.

"I'll tell you later. I need to check some things first."

I had a friend back in London who was a financial journalist. He knew about all this stuff and could get the low-down on Horace. I intended to phone him as soon as it was day in London.

A couple of the guys from the Joe Blows were in the bar. The Blows were a rhythm sextet that played some very bouncy stuff.

The musicians had been around for years but had struck lucky with the score to a TV show that had been a crossover hit.

Among the band-members was Otis's ex-wife Catherine, a gentle woman who played mean tenor saxophone.

I must say I was disappointed by the behavior of the musicians in the bar. I thought they would be draped over each other in a drug-, alcohol- and/or sex-induced haze. Then I realized these were the rock survivors—i. e. the dull ones. The squash players. The—yech—golfers.

"I've never used a Flymo," one was saying. "Maybe I should because I know I'm going to cut through the flex one day with my bloody thing. Can you get petrol driven ones? If the Flymo is anything like my current mower, the lead won't be long enough to get that bit at the bottom of the garden—you know, round the back of the rockery."

"What—the barbecue area? I thought that was paved?"

"No, next to there. Where the loungers are for that last bit of the day's sun. Six o'clock every evening in the summer the sun shines on there. We like to have a cup of tea there and put our feet up when I'm home, have a bit of a chin-wag. Debs, she's always planning some changes she is. She sez to me the other day she feels a Welsh dresser phase coming on."

Debs I knew was his wife, your standard rock-star wife—ex-page 3 girl from Penge turned baby-breeder.

"Off with the old and on with the new, eh?" the other guy said, though I wish he hadn't. I remembered seeing him in a punk band in the early eighties when he used to bite the heads off live chickens. "My Charlene is just the same."

Well, she would be—she was another ex-page 3 girl, though she was from Rickmansworth.

"Does Otis know about the death threats?" I said to Richard.

He gave me a sly look.

"D'you think we'd let him go onstage not knowing?" He grinned suddenly. "Actually it was under discussion. Horace was in agonies. Working out the losses on the tour if Otis didn't go on stage versus the losses if he wasn't around any more taking into account the royalties on the back catalogue if he kicked it."

"But there's no commercial money to be made on this gig is there? I assumed everything was for charity—you know, the drugs thing."

Richard gave me what could only be described as an old-fashioned look.

"Get real Nick. Nobody does anything for nothing. Sure money's going to the charities but nobody's going broke here. And Otis stands to make the most, which he definitely needs."

"I think Horace is skimming."

"I thought you thought that. But have you met a rock manager you couldn't accuse of that?"

"I guess."

Richard looked bored.

"What's this about Baza?" I said after a moment.

"Little bit of R & R before we hit Peru. Going up there tomorrow—it's an hour north of Bogota—then hitting the airport from there." He turned. "Ladies!"

Otis's two backing singers were standing beside us. One black, one close-cropped blonde, both beautiful.

"Nick, meet Sukie and Venus."

They nodded to me.

"How far is it from Cusco to Machu Picchu?" said Sukie, the blonde. "I was hoping to see the Nazi lines."

"Again?" Richard said.

"Nazca lines," I murmured.

"Those huge constructions that can be seen from the air?" the girl said—she had that Californian habit of turning every statement into a question. "In the shape of cows, chickens, and stuff?

"A dog, a monkey, a spider, and birds," I said.

"Whatever," she said with a pout.

Here we go again. More New Age nonsense. I knew about the Nazca lines. They'd been discovered by a German doctor who marked them out largely using a stepladder. Took her forty years, mind. She maintains they represent some sort of vast astronomical pre-Inca calendar. Personally I think it's just another example of the ways the Inca emperors got their subjects to pass the time before the invention of television.

"We've got a similar thing though much smaller in England called the Glastonbury zodiac," I continued. "You can see all the signs of the zodiac on a map of the area around Glastonbury."

"No shit," Venus said.

"But not because they are there, just because we have a capacity for making random markers into shapes, turning nothing into something, one thing into another."

Sukie and Venus joined us. Well, Richard really. The only remark Venus made to me was when she touched my face and told me it looked sore. Even I didn't believe that was the start of anything.

Richard took over. With a few drinks inside him he was outrageously laddish with women. I was appalled. The women, depressingly, loved it.

"I heard you two like to sing in harmony," he said with a leer. I flinched. They giggled.

Otis was over the other side of the bar with Ralph. Ralph was giving him a serious talking to. Otis looked mutinous but simply nodded.

"Where's Conchita?" I said to Richard, who at that moment had an arm round each of the singers.

"Out at dinner with her band and some big shot politicians."

I drifted away from Richard and the girls, saw Otis leave the bar. I had a couple of drinks with Perry, the *Rolling Stone* journalist. A skinny guy in tight black jeans and T-shirt, naturally, with sinewy arms, receding long grey hair pulled back into a ponytail, scraggly beard, and a sallow face.

I abandoned him when he was tying up some theory about pop music being more important than Marx. He was practicing on me before making it into an article, I could tell.

When I left the bar I realized I was drunk. Which is, I suppose, the reason I decided to visit the dance club again. And who should I see across the other side of the bar as I made my careful progress from the door but Otis.

It was pretty dark over there but there was no mistaking his brooding look. And he *was* brooding. The light shining down on him made him look so intense I decided not to go over.

I looked round for Ralph, couldn't see him. Otis was approached by a trio of squealing, sultry women, including the one I'd been dancing with the night before.

I was getting some hostile looks from the men in the room and, since my body seemed to want to tilt to the horizontal, I figured I should leave. The three women were still clustered around Otis. I looked round to see if the man from last night was also here, then I left.

So it wasn't until the morning that I heard what happened.

We were meeting at ten in the bar to get the convoy to take us on our R & R. I was talking to Richard—he wasn't speaking in anything but monosyllables and I could guess why, the lucky bastard.

Ralph came into the bar. Although he clearly didn't want to speak to us, the bar was too small to avoid it.

"You see Otis?" he said.

"Not since last night down at the club he was boogieing the other night. Great mover," I said. "Regular ole snakehips."

"Boogieing?" Richard tried the word out for himself. Frowned. "I don't think people still say that without irony, Nick. The eighties were a long, long time ago you know, kid."

"Last night?" Ralph said, ignoring Richard. "Time was this?"

"Midnight—why, has he got a curfew?"

"You saw him there?"

"Great mover," I said. "Regular ole snakehips.

"Never figured Otis for a dancer," Richard said.

"I tell you, for a man his size he can really move." I turned to Ralph. "But is there a problem?"

"Yeah there's a problem. He's not supposed to go out without his bodyguard. And never without using the bombproof car. He knows that."

Ralph left us without another word.

"I assumed the death threats were done with," Richard said.

"Apparently not," I said.

"I'd better check this out, too," Richard said.

I didn't see Otis, Ralph, or Richard before I was put in a minibus—excuse me, people carrier—with several other journalists and sent on my way.

We had two bodyguards with us. One was a young guy in T-shirt and denims, his gun stuck in a small holster at the back of his belt. The other, called Raoul, was around fifty and recently retired from the army where he'd been a sergeant major for twenty-five years.

It took us an hour to clear the city. We drove north, past the airport. The older bodyguard pointed out the castle on the right as we came to a large roundabout.

"A drug chief had it imported brick by brick from Spain and rebuilt here."

A mile or so farther on the left was a ranch guarded by tanks and jeep-loads of soldiers pulled up by the side of the road. The President's out -of -town retreat.

The other journos and I swapped war stories from that epic battlefield, the movie and rock industries. Perry sat with his head in a book.

There were about seven vehicles in our procession, all led by the outrider, who seemed little the worse for wear after yesterday's excitement. We turned on to a dirt road and for the next very bumpy hour hurtled in and out of a series of valleys until, in the final one, we followed a river through to the Hacienda Baza.

Getting out of the car and stretching my legs, I looked in astonishment at the beautiful 400-year-old Dominican monastery. I'd been reading up on it in a brochure. It had been in the family of the owner for generations. The family had turned it first into a ranch then an exclusive hotel with rooms for just twenty people.

It was very quiet—thick stone walls, high hills all around, lush gardens in cloisters. I was sharing my room with Richard. It was big and bare—tiled floor, high groined ceiling, and a fire hearth with a canopy over it, the chimney running up inside the wall.

The veranda that ran round the inside of the cloister was walled with exotic foliage and bright flowers. I'd only been in the room ten minutes before Richard turned up. He looked shattered.

"What's happening?" I said. "Is Otis okay?"

"Well, he's alive," Richard said, dumping his bag at the bottom of one of the beds and flinging himself down. "Ralph found him passed out on his bed."

"Is there a problem?"

"The problem is what he did at the club you saw him at last night. Didn't see him get into a rumble did you?"

"Three women were being friendly if that's what you mean by a rumble."

"Only where you're concerned. One of those girls has a guy. Guy got pissed off with Otis."

"I think I know him—Otis danced with her?"

"Apparently not—not drunk enough probably. Guy makes a fuss, Otis leaves, guy leaves with his woman half an hour later, Otis is waiting."

"Oops."

"Oops is right. Otis cold-cocks him."

"*Cold-cocks* him? Where do you get this lingo, Richard?"

"Seventies movies. Okay—beats the living shit out of him—swats the woman away. Now this is rather foolhardy since the Colombian gent, like most of the male population of Colombia, is packing. But Otis takes his gun off him, makes him suck it—"

"Otis must have seen the same movies as you—"

"Then walks off with the gun."

"Otis told you all this?"

"Club manager. Hope it doesn't mean Otis is back on the toot. It really fucks with him."

"So what's happening?"

"Ralph is down paying off just about everybody to keep it from getting in the press, to prevent Otis being arrested—whatever you want."

"And it's working?"

"We'll know later."

Richard went to bed. I went down to the bar—another high-ceilinged room, the walls covered with paintings, many of them painted by our host. Catherine, Otis's ex-wife, and Beatrice were sharing a swing bench sipping cocktails on the terrace outside.

I looked across the walled garden to the hills around us.

"Fancy doing your yoga practice with me?" Beatrice suddenly said. She pointed to the garden. "It would be lovely to do it there."

Was she being risqué or did she mean exactly what she said.
Sadly it was the latter.

"Sure," I said. "Meet you in ten minutes."

Okay, okay, the yoga. *Astanga vinyasa*—power yoga in the
States—brisk, gymnastic, flowing, almost constant movement,
unlike any yoga you've ever seen. I've been trying for several
years to get the hang of the simplest level—the Primary Series—
though there are five levels higher.

It's hard work and you find yourself in some very unlikely
positions. Sometimes at very inconvenient times.

Beatrice was supple from doing a different form of
yoga so she kept up pretty well. It was my own fault that
disaster struck as I tried to show off. I'd got myself in the
lotus position—legs crossed, feet resting soles up against my
inner thighs. Then I'd forced my arms down through the
non-existent gap between my thighs and my calves—are you
following this?—to place my palms flat on the ground. Then
I raised myself off the ground.

Frankly I've never understood this position. Even my sort of
yoga is supposed to bring inner peace, but staying in this position
any length of time—any time at all come to that—was agony.

Quite aside from the cessation of the blood supply to most
of the body, it was damned difficult to do. Just as I was lowering
myself back to the ground I heard a commotion from the bar.

"Where's the oik who says he saw me?"

Distracted, I fell over. Beatrice, who had been watching
me closely, squatted down and leaned over me, attempting to
untangle my arms and legs as Otis's hulking form came round
the corner. Ralph was at his side. They stopped in their tracks at
the sight of Beatrice crouching over me.

Ralph pointed.

"That gentleman there."

Otis shook his head.

"Yeah, well he's just pissed off because I decked him yesterday." He raised his voice. "I should leave him like that, love, I really frigging should."

"Hi again," I said brightly. Otis came and stood on one side of me, Ralph on the other. Otis's eyes were red-rimmed.

"You the guy who claims I was out at the dance club last night?"

"You wen' without me las' night you bastar.'" Conchita was standing on the bar terrace. She tossed her head. I felt sure she would run the whole gamut of stereotypical Latin spitfire emotions if she had a mind.

"I didn't go out," Otis said, flicking a finger towards me. "This guy says I did but he's a journalist—you know, truth-teller."

"I saw you," I protested. I felt vulnerable arguing from my trapped position. I had pins and needles in my arms and legs. Not to mention my feet.

"*Thought* you saw him," Ralph corrected from my right. I looked over. "Otis says he never left the hotel room."

"How you know, you had enough to drink you don't remember nothing anyway," Conchita expostulated—something I don't see every day.

"I saw you in this club downtown."

"Who was he with?" Ralph said. I glanced across at Conchita.

"Er … three fans last I saw."

"Yeah I know about his fans," Conchita called over. "Wiggle-ass types with one thing on their mind. Same thing on your mind, you asshole."

"Jesus, Conchita, can you just hold it down for five frigging minutes," Otis said wearily.

He looked at Ralph.

"I never left the hotel room," he said, but with less conviction.

"And I certainly didn't punch anybody out. And what about this gun I'm supposed to have taken? You find it in my things?"

Ralph shook his head.

"You probably dumped it," he said quietly. Then he addressed me. "Did you see an altercation with the guy you had trouble with the night before?"

I shook my head—no mean feat in my current position.

"Did you drink?" Ralph said. It seemed like they were going over familiar ground.

"What the fuck do you think?" Otis almost bellowed, his face reddening, a vein on his neck throbbing. "But I didn't go out last night!" He jabbed a finger at Ralph. "You told me I wasn't allowed to go out so I didn't. I stayed in my room like a good little scout. If you don't believe me check the contents of the mini-bar. As in—there ain't any."

"You did get drunk then?" Ralph said sharply.

"As a stoat. How many times do I have to tell you?"

"And you say you damaged your hand punching a wall?"

"I assume so, yes."

Otis slumped, the anger suddenly gone.

"What you mean if I was drunk how do I know what the fuck I did?" He shook his head. "I would have remembered." He looked almost pleading. "I would."

I finally saw Otis's manager at dinner. The Rock Against Drugs tour were the only guests so it was quite boisterous in what had once been a chapel. Beatrice was at a table with the rest of her band and the Joe Blows. On such occasions journalists sit below the salt. I was at the opposite end of the main table to Otis, who gave me the occasional baleful look. Richard was sitting between Sukie and Venus.

I watched Horace. He didn't talk to anybody much, just

focused on his food and a large amount of red wine. Once I caught him looking at me in a thoughtful way.

I thought there might be a bit of *ad hoc* musicality after dinner but everyone was tired. Otis and Conchita left first. Beatrice slipped from the room when my back was turned. I suspected there was rather a lot of casual pairing off to which I was not party and definitely not privy. Richard didn't come back to our room.

I could hear the various moans and cries of pleasure across the cloister during the night. Everyone was at it except me. I didn't even have my hardwood dolphin to hug—Bridget had taken an unaccountable fancy to it and kept it close by her in her handbag.

I got up with the dawn—what the hell else was there to do? There was a mist over the hills. The hotel had horses and we'd been invited to help ourselves if we wanted a ride. My last experience of horseriding hadn't ended too well when on the Sussex Downs. I'd started a cattle stampede.

But I fancied myself as a gaucho wearing chaps riding fast across the pampas, though I wasn't altogether sure what chaps were. Pampas either, for that matter. I went to the stable block. Not a chap in sight, nor a set of those things—are they boleros?—that are two balls on each end of a rope and you chuck it and knock people out. I was probably in the wrong country for that.

I chose the smallest horse. I didn't care that my feet were almost brushing the floor, I felt safer that way.

Riding out, I nodded at the guard at the gate and let the horse amble around the perimeter wall of the hacienda. I could hear the noises of the morning—music on some tinny radio in a shack halfway up the hillside, cocks crowing, the tonk of sheep bells, dogs barking. It was magical.

I was at that section of the wall immediately behind the bar when I was surprised to see a familiar figure coming through the wicker gate a couple of hundred yards away and hurrying into the trees.

I guided my horse over to the trees. A narrow path ran through them, curling up a slight incline. The figure was nowhere to be seen. I dismounted, tethered my horse to a low tree branch, and walked slowly up the path. I approached the top of the slope gingerly but the path twisted down the other side amongst a denser growth of trees.

I felt foolish skulking in the woods, even though I was trying to do my best Hawkeye impersonation. But we weren't out of Colombia yet and if there was to be an attempt on Otis's life from however unlikely a source, today would be the day.

The trees thinned about 300 yards farther along. I caught sight of the person I was following hurrying along the path.

A youth sitting astride a scooter was waiting at the edge of the trees. He could only be a *sicano*.

The figure stopped a couple of yards from him. Flitting from tree to tree I got to within thirty yards. I wasn't near enough to hear the conversation but they were speaking very intensely.

When I saw the money change hands I thought I should get back to my horse before I was spotted.

I hurried through the trees off the path, though keeping it in sight, rather less Hawkeye than lumbering elephant. I heard the rip of the scooter departing.

My horse was amiably cropping some weeds by the tree. I untethered her, climbed on her saddle, and wheeled her. At least, I tried to wheel her.

I yanked at her head, she yanked back. I nudged her with my knees, she dipped her head and carried on munching.

I can never do that clicking noise riders do with their tongues but I did my nearest approximation. The horse looked up at me disdainfully as if to say. What the hell was that supposed to be?

I wondered if there was a language problem—maybe

different countries had different physical instructions for horses. The saddle and stirrups were different here to England—cowboy style, the stirrups were much lower.

Perhaps a nudge with the knees meant stay here and keep feeding your face as those hurrying footsteps along the path come closer. I dug my heels in under her ribs. That, in my experience, means canter. In my horse's experience it meant set off like a rocket. She jerked her head up and dashed away.

I've been on a bolting horse before—see my earlier reference to the Sussex Downs. However, I was only on this one a matter of seconds before the small matter of a large branch caught me full in the chest and I somersaulted to the ground.

There may not have been much dignity in my fall but at least I managed to release my feet from the stirrups.

I was sitting in the long grass, gingerly turning my neck, when the hurrying footsteps down the path came to an abrupt halt in front of me.

I looked up. Smiled woozily.

"Hi, Conchita. Nice morning."

# TEN

Lima surprised me for three reasons. First, I thought it was up in the Andes so flying over a vast expanse of desert—half of Peru is sand—came as a shock, especially when we then ended up on the coast.

Second, Lima turned out to be a surfer's paradise, huge rollers crashing onto a long, long beach as regular as metronomes. I'd assumed in my racist way the city would be full of poncho-garbed men in knitted hats with earflaps and women wearing bowlers toddling around on llamas. But the part of Lima we were staying in was full of surf bums.

The third cause for surprise was that somebody tried to kill me. Surprise is perhaps too tame a word for the motion I expressed at this last. Shock takes us near the ballpark. Terror gets us through the gate. Why me? What was wrong with Otis?

There had after all been another warning for Otis that morning. When I took the horse back to the stables—when Conchita eventually caught it for me—the place was in an uproar, security guards running this way and that, Ralph on three phones and a walkie talkie.

Conchita slipped away in the confusion. I hadn't been able to find out what she was up to. The conversation had gone along the lines of:

"Hi, Conchita."

"Hi, Nick. Little early in the day for trick-riding, dontcha think?"

She strode past me as I stumbled to my feet.

"You're up early, too," I said before she thrust two fingers into her mouth and emitted an ear-splitting whistle. The horse, which had slowed to a walk some thirty yards away pricked up its ears and cantered obediently back.

Conchita swung easily into the saddle and smiled down at me, then started back to the hacienda at a trot. I found myself running alongside like the serf attending the lady of the manor.

"So you were taking a morning stroll, eh?" I called up to her as I puffed alongside.

She ignored me as she wheeled the horse round the corner to the front of the house. When I turned the corner she had reined the horse in. In front of the hacienda security guards were running around. On the windshield and bonnet of the armored Mercedes was the spray-painted message *Death to Otis Barnes*, except Death was spelt Deth.

"At least they knew the English words," I muttered but when I turned to Conchita she had slipped away and I found myself talking to the horse. Even she wasn't listening.

I didn't get a chance to talk to Ralph before he helicoptered Otis, Conchita, and Horace out. Nor was I sure what to say. Could the young thug on the scooter have spray-painted the car? How could anyone have spray-painted the car without the guards seeing since it was parked right in front of the hacienda?

Turned out there had been what Raoul, the older guard, called a "winnow of oppity" when the guard from the gate had left his post to see the last ten minutes of some big soccer match between rival Colombian sides on TV in the office.

He had still been able to see—and prevent—anyone coming through the gate or over the wall, which was, as far as he was aware, his main function. He wasn't worried about what might be going on outside.

Raoul told me this in the people-carrier on the way back along the dusty, bumpy road to the airport. I don't know what strings Ralph had pulled or who he'd paid off but we were whisked straight through and onto the plane without any of the usual formalities. Otis, Conchita, and Horace were already up in first. I was cattle class, naturally.

Two hours later we landed in Lima. We reached our beach-front hotel around two in the afternoon. All the rooms had great sea views apparently. Well, except mine. Depressingly, I accepted it as my lot. I did have a great view of the edifice that dominated the place—an advertisement in the form of a giant cigarette packet on stilts that seemed to tower over even the skyscrapers, visible all over the city.

Beatrice was in the hotel lobby. "You coming surfing?" she said. I couldn't figure her. I'd decided she wasn't a nutter but that therefore she wasn't interested in me in "that way."

"I'm not sure surfing is my thing," I said. No sport that involves standing on planks has ever struck me as a particularly rewarding or sensible activity. So the fact that I found myself ten minutes later not on a surfboard but a pair of water skis you can put down to a pathetic last-ditch attempt to impress the braided beauty on the next set of water skis along.

The Joe Blows and Fertile Lands were both on the beach, although I didn't see Otis's ex-wife Catherine. Benny the per-cussionist had apparently staked out a corner of the hotel bar for himself until the concert.

So there could be a live link with some satellite relay, the concert wasn't taking place until midnight—dinnertime here in Peru, which in common with other Latin American countries followed the Spanish tradition of going out for the evening when northern Europeans are happily tucked up in bed.

Picture a bronzed, young god skimming blue waters, one hand clasping the tow rope from the boat, the other raised in a negligent wave to his admirers on the beach. Now picture me.

The problem was getting up out of the water. You start out underwater, knees tucked against your chest, skis parallel, with only your head, shoulders and the tips of your skis above the water.

The boat takes off, the tow rope tautens, you rise out of the water, straighten up, and you're in business. Well, that's the theory. Me, I fell forwards, fell sideways, fell backwards, smacked myself on the nose with the skis—there's no dignity in these sports you know.

Eventually, though, the big moment. A perfect skiing posture and the boat pulled me almost a quarter of a mile—the first-ever underwater water-skier.

Beatrice was waiting for me when I finally staggered ashore, waterlogged.

"Nick—can you do anything right?" she said impatiently.

Good question actually. She stayed on the beach as the others were still surfing. I went back in the hotel to get rid of the gallon of seawater sloshing around inside me.

You use salt water in a yoga purification exercise not dissimilar to colonic irrigation. It has a remarkable effect on the digestive system—as I was to discover over the next few days.

I wasn't sure how to handle the Conchita thing. I could hardly say to Otis, 'I think your girlfriend is planning to have you killed,' especially as I didn't know who the guy was that she'd met. He could be another lover for all I knew. Maybe he'd spray-painted Otis's car, but there were plenty of other possibilities, too.

I decided I would tell Ralph—if I could get hold of him.

Left to my own devices—the alternative was hanging out with Perry to discuss the phenomenology of rock—I thought I'd do a little sightseeing in old Lima.

It's a big city, its population of 8 million representing a third of the population of the entire country. Since the country is twice the size of France, that means something statistically fascinating, but as the next page of my guide book was torn out I'll never know what.

I took a cab that dropped me off in the Plaza des Armas shaken and bruised. Shock absorbers were clearly regarded as a luxury in the cabs here. There was a socket for a seat belt but no actual belt so I spent the trip with my feet braced against the dashboard, which rocked alarmingly.

In the square, in front of the President's palace, young boys with long rifles slung down their backs hung around in groups whilst police and other paramilitary vehicles were lined up three deep facing the palace.

I walked down a narrow street towards the Church of San Francisco, past a string of tatty but atmospheric old shops—deep, high-ceilinged but selling only a few dusty wares. I passed a great-looking bar except there were only about three bottles on the rows of shelves behind the counter. A television was on the counter and all of the customers were engrossed in watching a football match.

Some kids wearing sandals and old plimsolls were playing football in the street. I heard the grind of gears and a whining noise behind me. One of the kids picked up the ball and they all moved without haste onto the pavement to let the tank go by. It trundled down the center of the street followed by a couple of foot soldiers. The kids didn't look twice, just went back into the road and carried on their game.

When I walked into the church I bumped into Catherine, Otis's ex-wife.

"Didn't expect to see a rock journalist in church—it's a bit late to beg forgiveness for your many sins."

"I would have thought that went double for a rock musician,"

I said. "But I'm not really a rock journo. I'm more your cultured type. I read there were some great Spanish tiles imported from Seville. I came to have a look."

Well, yes, that is my idea of a good time.

"They're in the cloisters," she said. "Unless you're a serious Catholic don't bother with the church itself—very baroque with horrible iconography—cheap dolls tricked out in tat to awe the peasants."

We walked up a flight of stairs to the cloisters. Off to the right was an extraordinary library of mouldering old books—the library of the original priests shipped over some five centuries before, then left to rot.

"Twenty or thirty monks still live here," Catherine said. "One of them is a medical monk—he gives free treatment to the poor of the neighborhood every week."

We were drifting through a long, shady length of cloister, the Seville tiles showing scenes from a monk's life high on the wall to our left. It was very still and sound refracted oddly. Our footsteps and those of half a dozen others also in the cloisters echoed loudly.

She was a pretty woman, in her early forties I guessed, her eyes and her mouth edged with laugh lines which deepened when she laughed, which it turned out she did easily. Her eyes were cornflower blue—well, the pupils were; she'd have looked a bit silly if the whole lot was blue.

"From all I've heard about you and Otis," I said, "I was expecting a victim, face turned to the wall."

"That was many years ago," she said, dragging back her hair with a long fingered hand. "But you should have seen me before the therapy. That really saved my bacon."

"So what do you think about Otis now?" I said as we descended a flight of stairs into the dimly-lit catacombs.

"I try not to think about him at all," she said with a small shudder.

I go off first appearances a lot—I'm trivial that way—and she didn't strike me as the kind of woman who would be sending threatening mail or spray-painting cars.

"Beatrice enjoyed the yoga," she said as we came to our first pit full of bones. I glanced at a notice high on the wall. This used to be the public cemetery, where 25,000 people were buried.

"You familiar with it?" I said as we reached an alcove some three feet deep, full to the brim with stacked bones, neatly sorted according to size. They were stylishly lit by concealed lighting below.

"I once did a tour with Sting. He was into it."

"Did you try it?"

"Too energetic for me."

She stopped and gave me an up-from-under look.

"I like things slow, languorous, and easy."

I blushed. Of course I blushed. But I held her gaze. Don't anybody tell me I can't handle women who like to play with their sensuality. I can't, but don't tell me.

We were standing on a sort of bridge. Below us on both sides were pits stacked with undifferentiated bones, skulls, all manner of remains of dead people.

And in racks on either side of us were yet more bones. One part of my brain was wondering what the hell place this was. The larger part (and we're still not talking much) was focussed on Catherine.

"Well sure," I said, still blushing furiously. "I'm the same. But this yoga is something else. You should really give it a try."

"Perhaps you could demonstrate it for me, too."

Again the smile at the corners of her mouth. She walked ahead and I paused to collect my thoughts. Since my brain felt like a colander this could well have taken some time. And would have, had I not heard a clattering sound above my head. I looked up in time to see the highest rack of bones to my left cascading down towards me. A moment later I was engulfed by them—skulls, thigh bones, rib cages, femurs—every manner of bone.

A moment later I was engulfed by them.

I can't imagine many people know what it's like to be on the receiving end of an ossuary. It hurts. Think about being kicked on the shin. Now think about being kicked *by* a shin. Any number of shins.

Bones that I didn't even know existed piled over me. I was battered to the ground and lay curled in the fetal position, my arms round my head as the bones continued to shower down.

Over the rattling of the bones of the former citizens of Lima I heard Catherine cry out. But did I also hear some echoing, receding male voice singing "Dem bones, dem bones, dem dry bones?"

I lay there for a moment, trying not to choke on the dust. Then I heard Catherine calling my name and the sound of bones being tossed aside. There was some space to flex my muscles. I flexed.

I wasn't exactly Venus rising from the foam but I did sort of explode out of the bones, sending them flying in all directions.

Dust clouds rolled off me. Catherine coughed, I choked.

"Are you alright?" she said then started to laugh.

I was less hurt than I expected, largely because the bones had formed a kind of tent over me.

"Aside from a nasty knock on the side of the head from a particularly pernicious femur and a poke in the eye from a sternum, surprisingly good—why are you laughing?"

"No reason," she said, covering her mouth with her hand.

I was pretty shaky and my head felt a bit weird—a tight feeling. Catherine helped me up the passage to the exit, occasionally pausing whilst I doubled over to cough and splutter.

The dust up my nose had joined with the seawater to form a kind of mud pack in my sinuses. Catherine occasionally patted me, sending puffs of dust from me.

"Did you hear singing?" I said as she started to giggle again. "What is it?"

"Nothing," she said, forcing a solemn expression onto her face. "They say that every breath we take contains minute particles of the breath of everyone who ever lived. So every intake of breath you get a bit of Hitler or Jesus or Mozart—"

I was racked by a sudden coughing fit.

"Bit of Stalin gone down the wrong way?" she said solicitously.

I'd expected some of the custodians to come running at the racket the bones had made but nobody appeared. I guess—and I apologize for this remark in advance—they were operating a skeleton staff.

I got some very odd looks when I emerged, I guess because I was covered from head to toe in grey dust.

"Did you hear singing?" I said again. My head was feeling so tight I wasn't sure if I'd imagined it.

"I did. Wouldn't let him in the band but maybe he could make a living on the pub circuit. Someone with a weird sense of humor, that's for sure."

"The same person who pushed those bones down on me," I said, ignoring the eyes swivelling towards me as we emerged in the sunlight.

"You think that someone did it deliberately?" Catherine said, waving at a taxi that was cruising by. "Bit paranoid aren't you?"

"Trust me—it happens in my life all the time."

The old Beetle Catherine had flagged down was even more decrepit than the one I'd come in. My door on the passenger side wouldn't close properly. This time I had a seat belt but nothing to clip it into—presumably the drivers shared the complete kit between them.

The gear stick wobbled alarmingly as the young driver

charged through the streets, maneuvering between big forties American cars.

He stopped for petrol before he took us out to the hotel—putting in a tiny drop, just enough for the journey. I wondered if he would leave the meter running—though that presupposed he had a meter, something I'd seen no evidence of.

Away from the main roads the streets were deserted. But in every bar we passed men were watching the TV with rapt attention. Our taxi driver paid us absolutely no attention, but then he was leaning half over into the passenger seat trying to listen to the football match on a tinny radio sellotaped to the dashboard.

He told us Peru were playing Uruguay. Driving back on the main road, he was hunched over his wheel, head dipped almost below the windscreen, weaving in and out of traffic. When Uruguay scored to make it 2-1 I thought he was going to drive straight into an oncoming bus.

My head felt no better and in consequence conversation between Catherine and I was minimal but there was a great deal of physical contact as we slid backwards and forwards along the back seat.

The taxi driver finally looked at me as I paid him off outside the hotel. As he set off almost collided with another taxi since he was looking back over his shoulder at me.

"Was my tip too generous or do I look really peculiar?" I said to Catherine.

She smiled and led me towards the mirrored facade of the hotel.

"Are you still hearing singing?" she said.

I started to reply, then caught sight of myself in the mirror and understood why. Fitted neatly round my head, like bleached bandanna, was a circle of bone.

Catherine let out a peal of laughter as she lifted it off my head.

"Better now?" she said, stroking my hair. "I'm sorry, Nick, but it looked so great planted there on your head."

I looked at it.

"You let me wear this—"

She gave me a hug and a kiss on the lips.

"I said I was sorry."

I turned it round in my hand.

"What is it anyway?"

"The ileum—half of the pelvic area."

"Should I take it back?"

She just grinned, then left me in the lobby to go for a soundcheck.

Nobody was around to observe me lugging a band of bone up to my room. I put it on top of the telly, brushed off my clothes and took a long shower, all the time turning over in my mind the things that were happening. Had someone tried to kill me?

But who could be after me? Horace, because he knew I had his papers? Conchita, because she guessed I'd seen her rendezvous with the young thing?

Benny was an outside possibility. He just might not have liked me asking questions about his relationship with Otis.

My money was on Horace, but only because I didn't like his socks—which I agree is not the best way to judge people.

Everyone was meeting for dinner in one of the restaurants on the beach before the concert. There was time for a yoga practice. It should have been great to be able to draw a full breath without feeling light-headed, but what with the dust and the water sloshing around in my sinuses, it was hard going.

When I got to the reverse postures—the headstand, handstand, and shoulder stand—I could feel this sludge shifting in my head and when I stood up a little trickle came down my nose.

The meal in the restaurant was par for this particular course, i. e. started well then sank into total chaos.

The restaurant was little more than a very large tent with wooden flooring laid down over the sand. At the end nearest the sea there was a clear plastic wall so that you could watch the waves roll in.

Otis was being remarkably sensible, drinking only Inca Cola, the drink of Peru. Some of the others, especially Benny, were hitting the pisco sours. I have no idea what they're made of but I knew from my own experience in Bogota that they went down very easily and made you suffer later.

We had an enormous meal of scallops followed by sea bass in olive oil. Everything seemed to be going smoothly, although I was catching glances from Horace, Conchita, and Benny all through the meal. Horace looked bored. Conchita smiled— complicitly?—and Benny smirked.

On his way to the toilet Benny stopped by my place and leaned over my shoulder.

"Hear you're a demon water-skier—ever thought of giving lessons?"

Fuck off was the expression that sprang unbidden to my lips but I merely smiled tightly. I've been insulted by experts. Often.

A roving trio of musicians were moving from table to table playing 'Latin American Ballads We Have Loved,' the vocalist getting a nice little throb of emotion in his voice.

Beatrice had just stopped by when the musicians approached Conchita and Otis.

"Catherine told me you had a bad experience in some catacombs today." I had a big lump on my forehead where I'd got a Glaswegian love bite from some fifteenth century skull. She touched it gently. "Are you okay?"

The trio struck up with a truly appalling version of John Lennon's "Beautiful Boy," about his son Sean when he was a baby.

"You think I look bad, you should see what's left of the

other guys," I said. Beatrice laughed and started to say something. I never heard what it was. There was a roar from the other end of the table.

Otis obviously didn't think much of the band's rendition either. I looked in time to see him rear from his seat and push the nearest band player hard. He fell against the singer's maracas—I know how cheap that sounds but he really did. The singer fell against the violinist. They toppled like skittles and I heard one of them squeak, which I took to be because the violinist's bow had gone somewhere it wasn't meant to be.

Otis picked up his chair, shrugged Conchita off, and raised it above his head to bring down on one or all of the hapless trio. As he did so a dozen flash bulbs went off.

Otis reared round and an unerring picture of King Kong came into my head. I spotted the photographers, virtually a wall of them, at the same time that Ralph wrestled the chair expertly from Otis's hands and hustled him firmly away.

At the same moment Richard jumped up from the table.

"Get their frigging films," he shouted to no one in particular. A moment later he was herding the photographers with the help of our security man into a corner, despite their resistance and the very vocal intervention of the maitre d'.

I saw one photographer head for the exit. Richard gave chase, but whether by accident or design—who knew who was on the take here—one of the waiters got in his way and the guy was out the door and away.

Richard threw up his hands and went back to the other photographers. It was bedlam over there. The security guys were trying to get the cameras, the photographers were holding them off, everybody was bellowing.

It was only a matter of time before somebody pulled a gun and my worry was it was going to be one of our guys.

I went over to Richard and touched his arm. He ignored

me, so I gripped harder. He swivelled, fist balled and ready to punch me. Seeing me, he held back.

"Fuck, Nick, not now. Can't you see I got a situation here."

"Yeah, and you're handling it all wrong."

"I can't let these guys leave here with their film. These pictures get published and we're in deep doo-doo. This was a frigging set-up."

"Even so you can't do it—these guys were going about their legitimate business."

"This is no time to go into a freedom of the press spiel. We're here as guests of the President's wife. She sees us abusing her hospitality, we got a major diplomatic incident."

"She hears how you worked over her press you got worse—because if they turn against her because of this she'll really be pissed off."

Richard paused in his attempts to drag a camera from round the neck of the nearest photographer, which was just as well since the guy was choking on the strap and only seemed to have a few more seconds of breath left in him.

"What do you suggest?"

"You've got to let it go, man. Let them go." I reached over and prised his fingers off the guy's camera. "Contain it some other way. Get Conchita over here now to calm things down—everybody adores her. Then do what you do best—hit the phones the minute these guys are out the door. These pictures won't be in the press until tomorrow. The President's press corps will be on duty all night—talk to them."

Richard was quick, I'll give him that. "Bring Conchita," he said to one of the security guys. "How do you say 'sorry' in this language?"

I waded in with Richard to placate the photographers, the waiters, the other diners. Conchita came over and did the rounds, we ordered up champagne for the diners, handed out free concert tickets to the waiters and the snappers.

Later, Richard and I walked back to the hotel together.

"So how do I contain it? Christ, you can see the headlines: Rock Star Guest of President's Wife Attacks Local Musicians In Drunken Rage. We're meant to be about peace and love, man. Peace International are going to freak when they hear about it, too."

"That headline is way too long," I said absently. Then: "I didn't know the President's wife was supporting the tour."

"It's been kept hush-hush but it was going to be announced at the gig tonight."

"She's going to be there?"

"Not here. Machu Picchu. *Was* going to be there."

"What makes you so sure it was a set-up?"

"If it wasn't, it was a very, very unfortunate coincidence them playing 'Beautiful Boy.'"

"So badly, too."

"I don't think it was the quality of the performance Otis objected to—Nick, have you been taking prescribed drugs you're not telling me about? Your reaction is a bit odd."

"Sorry, it's been a bit of a giddy day one way and another. What's the problem with 'Beautiful Boy?'"

"You've heard his recording of it from way back?"

"Sure. Great."

"Recorded it for his son Paul."

"I didn't know he had a son Paul."

"Not many people do—the mother wanted it that way. Ever wondered why he never ever plays it on stage, it never turns up on his best-of CDs?"

"I'm wondering now."

"He recorded it; the week the album came out mother and child were killed by a hit-and-run driver. Guy was never caught. Otis was devastated."

"I didn't know."

"Hardly anybody does, which is why if it's a set-up it's been done by somebody who knows him very well."

I let that go for a moment as we entered the foyer of the hotel.

"You've got to tell the President's wife, get her press corps to tell the press."

"He's kept it secret all these years."

I shrugged. "The secret's out and you might as well milk it. Get the sympathy vote."

There was a sudden gleam in Richard's eyes. Told you he was quick.

"You're right, you're right. Nick, I owe you. I've got to go and work the phones. I'll catch you later."

He hurried away leaving me alone to ponder what I'd observed immediately after the fracas at the restaurant had erupted. Horace, part way down the table, glancing up then continuing to eat his sea bass as if nothing was happening. And Benny, leaning against a pillar, across the room from the toilet he'd been supposedly heading for, a gleeful look on his sallow face.

# ELEVEN

I lay on my bed for half an hour then locked myself in the bathroom for another half hour—the salt water was having a deleterious effect upon my person. I got in the lift to the lobby at around eleven. I'd been mulling over the different things that had been happening. Call me selfish but I was more concerned for the moment with the threat to my life. The lift stopped at the second floor and the doors opened.

Horace stepped in. He had his hands in his pockets and he was wearing a white linen suit with black brogues. I wanted to say, "No!" but before I could worry more about his sartorial ineptness he leaned towards me and said in a sinister voice, right out of some British black and white B movie from the fifties:

"You got something of mine?"

He was standing toe to toe and looking up at me. Given the disparity of our heights my immediate thought was to wipe my nose, just in case. My second thought was that I hope he didn't have X-ray eyes or he'd see the documents in question in my side pocket.

I wondered for a moment if he was going to try some rough stuff. It didn't seem likely but maybe he'd heard what a pushover I was.

"Have I?" I finally said. I know it wasn't much of a response but I still had bits of dead people in my gums, possibly thanks to him.

Before he or I could say more the lift reached the ground floor and the doors sprang open. Horace half turned.

"Just coming looking for you," Bridget said.

Horace looked from her to me then stepped out of the lift.

"Nasty bruises," he called back as he headed for the door.

"Shit, yes," Bridget said, giving me a hug as I stepped out of the lift. "Who've you been upsetting?"

"Do you want the list?" I said.

"Let's just put it down to another disappointed lover shall we?" she said.

"No, listen, Bridget, there's some bad stuff going on here."

"With you around, when isn't there?"

"Help me out tonight, will you?" I said. "Things could get hairy."

"Yeah, yeah," she said. "Let's get going."

The taxi was a lot better than the one I'd taken earlier, until I noticed the cigarette in the driver's mouth.

"Oh God," I said, "he's smoking."

"So?" Bridget, who is always quitting tomorrow, said testily. "The window's open."

"Roll-ups," I said.

Bridget didn't get it until the driver was overtaking on the first bend. Overtaking on a bend is in itself a little foolhardy. Rolling a cigarette two-handed at the same time ...

As best I could, I filled Bridget in on what had been happening. I'm not sure how much attention she paid, clinging to me as she was.

When we reached the stadium, there was a bit of hassle getting her in. Security was tight.

"Don't they know who I am?" she said grandly.

"Not a clue," I muttered.

I had to get Ralph along. He came down in his usual bad mood but, credit to the guy, he did sort it.

"Chaos tonight," he said. "Even Otis lost his pass, needed a new one."

I felt I could trust this guy —aside from Richard, probably the only person on the tour that I could.

"Ralph, we need to talk about what's happening," I said.

"We got nothing to say to journalists."

"I'm not after a quote, you dufus—"

"Dufus?" I could almost hear his muscles ripple.

"I want to talk to you about who's doing all this."

"I told you—nothing to say to journalists."

With hindsight of course it was foolish of me to get hold of his shoulders and try to shake him.

"Look, I've got information might be useful," I said in a Minnie Mouse sort of voice. I was backed against a wall, his hand tight on my windpipe, his knee thrust between my thighs poised to do me serious and probably permanent damage.

"That'd be a first," he said, before suddenly releasing his grip and sinking into a crouch.

"Pick on people your own size," Bridget said to him, pulling her hand from between his legs. She tottered off on her high heels, calling back over her shoulder: "And thanks for the pass."

"Ralph," I said as he crouched there. "I really do have some useful info." He was remarkably big about it. He took me into an office and, as the Joe Blows opened the gig, I told him about, well, everything.

That's to say: Conchita's secret meeting, Horace's paperwork, Billy's smirk at the restaurant.

He was a bright guy, he didn't need it spelled out.

"I'll get back to you," he said, sliding from the room.

I lost Bridget early in the night. So much for her helping me out. I hung out at the side of the stage for a while watching

Catherine do her bit with the Joe Blows. She had a couple of nicely judged solos, one blowsy and sassy, the other slow and melancholic.

I was getting another beer from the green room when Ralph and Conchita appeared at my elbow. She was in her stage costume—a short backless, damned near frontless, electric-blue dress.

"I theenk you and I have a misunderstanding to clear up."

I waited for her to say more.

"In Baza, the person I was talking to was my brother."

"He looked like a—"

"I know what he looks like. And he is. He fell into bad company. My stepfather, he's involved. I try to get him to see sense but he don't want to. He likes the life."

"The money you're earning, can't you—"

"Buy him out of the business? He don't want out and he don't need money. If he survives he'll make more than me."

"But it means you're compromised," Ralph said.

"Everybody is compromised on this fucking continent," Otis said. He had come up quietly behind me. "Man, don't you get it? Everybody is on the take. The other year the Peruvian police arrested two high-ranking navy officers for running cocaine shipments to Europe on navy ships.

"Can you imagine? The frigging navy. These guys packed 220 lbs of the powder apiece in the engine rooms of their ships in the harbor at Callao. Every trip to Europe they dropped the stuff off in whatever port they docked in.

"And God knows why the police arrested them, since most of the security forces are involved in drug trafficking anyway. So these guys were arrested for justice? I don't think so—probably they poached on somebody else's patch.

"Shit," he went on, "these guys even use the President's own jet, a Peruvian Air Force DC8, to smuggle toot. A while back the police hauled 38 lbs of the stuff off it. Ten senior air force officers were about to set off on a goodwill tour of Europe—that's the kind of goodwill people understand. These people been doing it for years—regular flights to London, then Amsterdam they were offloading the stuff."

"What's your point?" Ralph said. "That this tour's a waste of time?"

"Man I lost friends to drugs," Otis said. "I damned near killed myself with them—though that would have been no tragedy." I was startled by the self-contempt in his voice. "This tour is—you gotta try, you know."

"And what's this got to do with the Conchita situation?"

"She was running an errand for me," Otis said. He saw Ralph's face.

"Not drugs. I'm through with them. Information." Otis shook his head and looked back at Ralph. "Don't you think I know what's going on? All these whispered conversations, hustling me away at short notice. One of these jokers sending death threats is *really* out to get me right?"

"It's a possibility," Ralph said.

"Well, fuck 'em, they can't brace me face to face, got to send threats. Ain't gonna stop me going on stage. Times I feel a bullet in the brain would be very welcome."

"Otis!" Conchita wailed.

"Sorry, baby, but it's the truth. Anyway, I wanted to find out who it was likely to be. Conchita's got her brother to check around."

"I saw her hand over money," I said.

"Sure, he had to pay people. Kid's a businessman—wasn't going to use his own money."

"And?" Ralph said.

"Only got negative stuff. No drug baron is that interested. The right wing death squads huff and puff but they aren't planning anything."

"So who sent the *sicanos* into Bogota stadium?"

"Don't know. Nor about the intentions of any guerrillas."

"Did Porras's name come up?" I said.

Otis shook his head.

"And nobody knows where he is. Freddy's gone to ground."

Richard came into the green room at this point. He came over with a cocky grin on his face.

"It's sorted," he said triumphantly. "Every paper's going to lead with Otis's sob story—pardon my French, Otis."

Otis glared at him then at me.

"Seems I've got to thank you for revealing my secret to the world's press."

"Otis, it would have come out sometime," Richard said. "Might as well make some use of it."

"Spoken like a true PR," Otis said sourly.

Conchita touched my arm. "I gotta go do my spot. Thought I should fill you in."

She sashayed away across the room.

"Do you have any more for me?" I said to Ralph. He shook his head.

"Not yet."

When Ralph had gone Otis looked at me.

"You're not the prat you first appear, are you, Madrid?" he said gruffly, before lurching away.

"Well done," Richard said, beaming like a proud father.

"For what?"

"You've won him over. He regards you as a mate."

"That's him being matey?"

Richard sighed.

"You don't know the half of it. Listen, Nick, I got a job for you."

"I've got a job thanks."

"I mean a proper job."

"It is a proper job."

"Journalism? Gimme a break. This is the real thing—glamour, adventure, riches beyond your wildest dreams."

I waited.

"I want you to watch Otis's back."

"He's got bodyguards."

"He needs another one."

"Me, a bodyguard? I do yoga."

"So?"

"Skip it. Why me?"

"You look stupid but you're not actually quite as stupid as you look—that gives you an edge."

"Thanks very much."

"Nobody else can seem to figure out what these death threats mean, so I just need somebody to keep their eyes open."

"But Otis is on some kind of death trip anyway—he's on self destruct."

"So help the guy help himself."

"I'm no good at rough stuff," I said, which is true.

"I've seen your knuckles mate."

I looked down at the scar tissue on my knuckles, straightened my shoulders, and sucked my stomach in.

"You having a spasm?" Richard said solicitously.

"Okay, I'll do it. What the hell—somebody's got it in for me, too."

I looked at my knuckles again. I didn't like to tell him they'd got like that diving into the shallow end of the White City swimming pool. Brought tears to my eyes thinking about it.

When the Fertile Lands came off stage Beatrice came over.

"Listen Nick, there's something I need to say."

The tone of voice was one I was accustomed to.

"You know, I thought maybe you and I ..."

"Yes," I said, trying to keep the fading hope out of my voice.

"The thing is, I need someone to look after me not—I can't be a nursemaid." She leaned over and kissed me on the top of my head. "Sorry."

"Make my day why don't you?" I muttered as she walked back to the rest of the band.

Benny smirked at me. I was pretty sure he was involved in the set-up at the restaurant. He would have known about Otis's son since they were in the band together around that time. But did he do it for spite or was he up to something more sinister?

I wandered back to the side of the stage. I was half looking for Catherine. Instead I found Ralph.

"I'm grateful for your assist earlier," he said. "Sorry I got a little rough, though your friend—Bridget is it?—paid me back in spades." He put his hand to his crotch gingerly. "I intend to brace Benny later. If he was behind the stunt at the restaurant he's on the next plane out."

Conchita's band started up with their infectious dance rhythm. Loud infectious dance rhythms. Ralph pulled me backstage and into one of the offices. He still needed to shout in my ear.

"But as for the other situation, I'm not sure what I can do about it. It comes under the heading of private business between Otis and Horace. I'm just a hired hand here. You're going to have to sort that."

"I'm waiting for a guy to call me back from London," I shouted. "Can't really do much until then."

"Something else," Ralph said. He had his pissed off look again. "As I said, I'm grateful for your assist. But I got Richard telling me he's asked you to watch out for Otis."

"He asked me to do that, yes."

Ralph opened the office door and looked out. He indicated two guys by the stage. One around six feet, pressed jeans, open-necked white shirt, slim, balding, curly-haired with a sad expression on his long face. He looked a nice guy, even with the handgun tucked into the front of his jeans.

"Hired them this morning specifically to shadow Otis."

"I'm no expert," I said, "but that gun seems too small for the job in hand. I gestured in the guy's direction. I mean it's probably very precise but can it do the big jobs?"

Ralph sighed and gave me a long look.

"You're right—you are no expert. You've heard of William Tell?"

"Of course."

There was a fruit bowl on a stand nearby. Ralph reached over and handed me an apple.

"Okay, stick that on your head, go stand over there. Jose there will shoot it off your head."

"That precise, huh?"

"There's no doubt in my mind the apple will be destroyed," he said, "but perhaps I should rephrase the remark. I know the gun can destroy the apple because I know it will take your whole head off."

I looked again at Jose.

"So what you're saying is I'm not needed."

"Correctamundo."

"But I'm not intended to provide the brawn—I'm the brain."

Ralph took a hurtfully long time to stop laughing. Then he leaned over and tapped me lightly on the chest.

"I'm the brain—don't you forget that."

At the end of Conchita's set she read out a statement from the President's wife. I didn't know enough about Peruvian politics to know how popular the President and his wife were but the message of support for the tour seemed to come across okay.

Otis took the stage to great applause. I was wondering where Bridget had disappeared to when Catherine joined me.

"Do you want to see the old man again, or do you fancy going out to a bar? It's only a couple of blocks away."

I don't get offers like that every day—any day actually.

"Sure," I said, impressed she'd already checked out the bars.

We flashed our passes to get out—that's what I call security—and she led the way down chilly streets to a retro chrome and leather place called The O Bar.

"What'll it be friends?" the barman said in an American accent. "Neat or through water?"

Ah shit—an oxygen bar. I'd seen a couple in Canada and one in New York but I'd read that someone was developing a franchise of them. Didn't serve booze, served oxygen at around ten quid a snort.

"Wanna gas up?" Catherine said to me.

"Take it here at the bar, or we have a private spa room through the back for a coupla bucks extra," the barman said.

Catherine looked at me.

"Here's fine," I said.

I'd sworn I'd never come in a place like this. It just seemed a really dippy fad. All you did, you inhaled 99 percent pure oxygen for twenty minutes through a tube into your nostrils. You could talk and drink your fresh juice. You got a great buzz but it was all self-induced—inhaling pure oxygen has no health benefits at all.

"Lemme just check your heart rate," the barman said, attaching a metal clamp to each of our wrists in turn.

"What happened to the bars where all you got in the way of extra service was a bowl of peanuts?" I said to Catherine nervously.

She smiled patiently. I was nervous because we'd been at high altitude coping with less oxygen and now presumably in coastal Peru our blood was positively bubbling with the stuff. Although I'd never heard of such a thing, I was worried I might OD on it.

"I've heard Mick takes a hit before a concert," Catherine

said. "Reckons it gives him energy for all the dancing around he does."

"Have you been in these places often?" I said.

She gave me an arch look.

"Don't think you've got the phrasing quite right, have you, Nick?"

I liked the way she said Nick, lightly. These things matter.

"I went to a wedding reception in Los Angeles in one of these places," she said. "Oxygen and fruit cake for 200 guests."

"Fruit cake is right," I muttered, looking round the bar at the dozen or so people sitting with clear tubes stuck up their noses.

"Sorry?" she said.

The barman came back before I needed to respond.

"The blast lasts twenty minutes. Do you want it plain or passed through a tumble of flavored water?"

"You decide," I said quickly.

"Plain for me," she said. "With an orange juice."

She looked at me. I nodded. "Make that two."

"Let me just give you your cannula here," he said.

He placed a kind of yoke around each of our necks. Each had a single tube leading to an oxygen tank behind the bar, and two smaller tubes that went up our noses.

Part of me was hoping the whiff of oxygen would sort out the water in my sinuses from my ducking in the Pacific—was it only earlier today?

The barman brought the fruit juices.

"Cheers," Catherine said, chinking glasses. Then she leaned towards me. "So tell me Nick, you seem to be a person in the know—what's going on with all the security around Otis and all these weird incidents?"

She had a very caressing voice—and she knew it.

I gazed deep into her eyes. Nice eyes, one either side of her nose, which is how I like 'em. I took another hit of oxygen.

"I can't say much," I said.

"Sure you can. Is it just Otis or the whole tour that's under threat?"

"Otis," I said.

"That's alright then," she said with a big smile.

I took another hit and a moment later saw the smile on her face freeze into a rictus, then her nose wrinkle in disgust.

With the last inhalation I'd suddenly felt the pressure in my sinuses relax. In the mirror behind the bar I saw thick fluid streaming from my nostrils.

I ducked my head and almost fell off my stool fumbling for a handkerchief. I was wiping my nose when Benny crashed through the door and headed straight for me.

I started to get up—only to be yanked back to my seat by the yoke round my neck, which was attached by the other end of the tubes to the oxygen tank behind the bar.

Just as well since it meant his first punch went wide. He didn't look the kind of guy who would have many punches in him but I wasn't taking any chances. I kneed him in the groin—something I'd learned from Bridget. She'd been educated at a convent so could have got odds on a bout with Sonny Liston. By accident—those damned tubes jerking my head forward—I also headbutted him full in the face.

He went down. Catherine jumped to her feet, throwing her yoke off, and ripping the tubes from her nostrils as the barman, calling "Hey," started over from the far end of the bar. She grabbed my hand and lunged for the door as I got rid of my yoke and the tubes finally pinged out of my nostrils—which hurt actually. We exited the bar at speed.

"God, this is just like the old days with Otis," she said breathily, dragging me into a shop doorway as I frantically wiped my nose with more tissues.

As she pressed herself against me I remembered she'd been

married to a thug—was there a part of her that was excited by violence? I thought I should tell her that I wasn't really like that, that in fact I abhorred violence. But as she began to caress me more ardently I thought perhaps I'd tell her in the morning.

# TWELVE

Benny was out of there the next day, shipped back to Britain on the first available flight. Richard told me this over breakfast. He looked exhausted—pale and hollow-eyed.

"I see your attempts to do justice to the generosity of Sukie and Venus are beginning to get to you," I said as I tucked into an unlikely breakfast of beans on toast—did I choose the hotel?

Richard gave me a long look.

"From what I hear," he finally said, "you're playing from a weak hand commenting on someone else's sexual capacity."

I laughed. But then I was feeling great. My night with Catherine had been extraordinary. She'd obviously been around the track a few times but I like to feel I provided some surprises. I was thrilled when she said she'd never experienced sex quite like it. So thrilled that whilst I've never been kiss-and-tell I felt the need to share it with someone the moment I was back in my room.

"And she said she'd never experienced sex quite like it—quite a compliment, don't you think?" I'd said.

"*Si*. But if you excuse me, sir, I must clean your bathroom," the chambermaid had replied.

Richard tapped the newspaper beside his plate.

"As it happens I'm tired because I spent most of the night sorting out the newspapers. It helped we could run with the

Benny story. Ralph braced him last night. Benny tried to tough it out but you don't out-tough Ralph."

He gave me a complicit grin.

"He looked a little the worse for wear this morning. Last night he was mouthing off about how he was going to be looking for you. Guess he found you."

I shrugged and took another mouthful of baked beans.

"You're a dark horse," he said. "Yes, you are."

"What are Fertile Lands going to do without their percussionist?"

"Get another one. What's a percussionist but a drummer with pretensions? And drummers are ten a penny in any city. The main thing is we can stop worrying about any more threats to Otis."

"You think Benny was behind all of them?" I said, surprised.

"Well, no, not back in Colombia. You know Otis's rule of thumb—why piss off one person when you can piss off a dozen? And he did piss people off there but we turned some of them around and now we're out of there."

He tapped the paper again.

"With luck this is the last thing we have to worry about. Even Conchita's being lovery-dovey with him—they came straight back to the hotel last night after the concert and Otis was *relatively* sober."

"That's great but Otis has a little problem with Horace."

My phone call had come through this morning and the conclusion my pal drew was that Horace had been draining Otis for years—the good years and the bad.

"Happens all the time in rock," he said, his voice unexpectedly loud down the phone line from London. "Remember when someone had been ripping Sting off to the tune—ha, ha—of a couple of million and Sting hadn't noticed because he had so much money going through his accounts?"

"I don't think Otis is in that league, Mark."

"Sure, but Horace has been doing very nicely, thank you."

I relayed this to Richard and named the sum Mark, my contact, estimated Horace had creamed off Otis.

"That buys a lot of Elvin the Elfin socks," I said.

Richard clamped my arm.

"Well, good luck."

"What do you mean?"

"Well I don't envy the person who has to tell Otis this."

"But—"

"And it ain't going to be me, pardner. You've got the scoop on this—it's your exclusive and you're welcome to it."

"Are you suggesting we might have a shoot-the-messenger scenario here," I said with a sinking heart.

Richard grinned.

"How'd Horace hitch up with Otis in the first place?" I asked.

"Horace was organizing gigs at universities along the south coast. When Otis was going down for the third time in the mid-eighties Horace offered a life raft. They're very different but it seems to work. Seemed to."

After breakfast I went back to my room and phoned Bridget. I hadn't seen her since I got her backstage pass at the concert the previous evening. There was no reply, not even "Fuck off," her customary greeting when her sleep is disturbed after a late night.

I phoned Catherine. I told myself it was to check on how to approach Otis with the bad tidings but it was really because I wanted to see her again. I told her about Horace.

"How should I approach it?"

"From a great distance," she said. "Otis has many faults, as I can be the first to testify. But aside from sexual fidelity he's very loyal to people. Once you get his trust, you've got it for life. Whether you want it or not."

She sounded sentimental.

"You still care for him?"

"I still love the bugger, sure. But I couldn't live with him without murder becoming a distinct possibility." There was a pause then she said. "Look, my advice, for what it's worth, is just tell him straight."

"Maybe I can talk to you about this later."

"Sure," she said.

"Will I see you later?"

"We're all on the same plane to Cusco, aren't we?"

"I didn't mean that," I said, dropping my voice into a lower register.

"Have you caught a cold?" she said. I listened to the static on the line for a moment then she continued: "Nick I like to live for the moment, and last night …"

"Had its moments?"

"Moment actually," she blurted, then quickly added. "Who knows what might happen further down the line? Nick, love, I'll see you at the airport. Good luck with Otis."

She broke the connection and I sighed before I put the phone gently back on its rest.


Cusco, the old Inca capital high in the Andes, is where things began to get really complicated. The flight up from Lima was uneventful. I was hoping to sit with Catherine but Bridget took the seat next to her. Every so often during the flight I'd be aware of the pair of them looking my way and sniggering.

I was stuck with Perry wittering on about the Incas.

"I don't see what the big deal is," he said. "First off you think 'Wow!' look at these huge cities and temples made out of these big slabs of stone. And sure they're impressive. You think Egypt and the pyramids. But dig, man, the Egyptians had done it a couple of thousand years earlier.

"These Incas and the damned Aztecs were running around in loincloths chopping the hearts out of virgins and sacrificing bodies whilst you Europeans were having your Renaissance. Here are your Stone Age dudes living in the fifteenth century.

"No wonder you got drug barons fighting each other and your general lawlessness in South America now—on their time-scale they've only just reached the Middle Ages. I tell you, the sooner they wake up and smell the twentieth century the better for all of us."

I made the mistake of arguing with him.

"I think you're ignoring their achievements. Just because they went around in loincloths doesn't mean they were savages. And there's no real proof of human sacrifice I don't think. Remember they had no written language so all the accounts we have of them are by Spanish conquerors. You know what they say: history is written by the victors."

"The conquistadors—you got it right there man. The Inca empire spread from Chile to Colombia. These guys so frigging advanced how come they got conquered by Mister Francisco Pizarro with 179 men and a couple of horses?"

"The Spanish arrived during a civil war."

But Perry wasn't having any. On and on he went until in desperation I put on my headphones and pretended to watch the inflight entertainment, an old movie about a bunch of astronauts lost in space.

The plane landed before the astronauts did. The film kept rolling so those passengers who wanted to see how the movie ended stayed in their seats to find out. Since this plane was due to make the return flight to Lima virtually on turnaround I could see how advertised plane times were only rough guides.

I waited until Perry had disembarked then followed.

Back in the rarefied air—we were just over 11,000 feet above sea level—I could see the difference in the quality of the light. There were even higher mountains all around, some capped with snow, some wreathed in mist or white clouds, others clear and acutely defined against the intense blue sky.

I watched Otis and Horace talking together, Otis with his arm round the much smaller man. Richard drew my attention to a slight dilemma for the tour in the airport concourse. To help adjust to the altitude new arrivals were encouraged to drink a cup of coca leaf tea, available from several stalls.

"We have an ethical problem here," Richard said,

I was startled. Not because there was a problem but because Richard knew the word ethical.

"We're the Rock Against Drugs tour but here we are faced with coca leaf from which cocaine is made."

"No problem," Otis said, looking back over his shoulder. "Coca isn't a narcotic, it's a stimulant. Cocaine is just a derivative of the leaf."

He picked up a packet of coca leaf tea from the stall.

"I don't know what happens when you make tea, but in its natural state the leaf has some fourteen alkaloids and a handful of vitamins in it. Chew the leaf and it gives a lift when the going gets tough.

"Maintains blood sugar level when protein intake is low, regulates the heart rate during drastic changes in altitude. Even dulls the appetite. But it ain't gonna get you stoned unless you chew half a trees worth of leaves."

Ralph spirited Otis and Horace away in a big Mercedes taxi. Bridget sidled up to me.

"There speaks a rock star—they have, in my experience, unequalled pharmacological knowledge."

I took a sip of the tea. It was bitter. I waited for some spinach/Popeye reaction on my body. In vain.

"I was hoping to sit next to Catherine on the plane," I said.

"Tough," Bridget said. "I would stay away from her for a while. Let her recover."

"She told you then?"

"Naturally. I'm pleased you managed to get laid at sea-level by the way, so there was no shortness-of-breath problems."

"No problems at all," I said. I ducked my head closer to her ear so that I could whisper. "I'm not one to boast but she said she'd never had sex quite like it."

I thought perhaps Bridget had swallowed her tea down the wrong way. She seemed to be choking. It took me a moment to realize it was suppressed laughter.

"You took that for a compliment did you?" she finally gasped.

Before I could wonder what she meant, Richard rejoined us.

"Had a word with Otis. Told him you had something to tell him. Seven o" clock in the hotel bar."

The taxi ride into Cusco took only ten minutes or so. Cusco was little more than a town but had within its narrow paved streets a phenomenal amount of Inca masonry. But then it had been the capital of the last Inca (Inca was the name of the leader of the tribe of Indians we now know as Incas).

I told Bridget: "In Cusco almost every central street has the remains of Inca stonework serving as the foundations of a modern home." I pointed to a distinctive Inca wall as we waited at a traffic light.

"Look. The stonework tapers upwards and every wall has a perfect line of inclination towards the center from bottom to top …"

Bridget blew cigarette smoke into my face.

"It was a mistake to let you sit with Perry," she said flatly.

We stopped in front of an old wooden gateway on a steep, narrow alley scarcely big enough for the taxi to drive along. Once through the gateway we entered a large luxury hotel built around two cloisters.

It had once been a monastery—Cusco has a remarkable

number of colonial churches, monasteries, and convents alongside or on top of its Inca ruins.

I had a room to myself so once I'd unpacked I spent the
time before my meeting with Otis doing my yoga very slowly. It
reminded me of Beatrice.

I went down to the bar at seven. It was small, with pre-
Columbian artifacts on display in alcoves lit from below. Otis
was already waiting there, a glass or so into a bottle of wine.

"So, Mr. Madrid, at last we meet," he said in some mock-
espionage voice.

He poured me a glass of wine as I settled myself facing him.
He'd taken his dark glasses off for a change—he might well
have missed the glasses otherwise. He looked fit and healthy,
despite the awesome amounts of alcohol he seemed to have
been putting away.

He raised his glass and looked me in the eye.

"To my ex-wife Catherine," he said in a gentle voice. "Who
I hear you're having carnal knowledge of."

I put my glass down. He saw the look on my face. I didn't of
course but I hoped it was suitably steely and square-jawed.

"Petulance doesn't suit you, pal," he said. "Personally I don't
care who you fuck but you've got some big shoes to fill there—
my shoes—and looking at you I don't see how you can."

"Are you really so obnoxious?" I said without thinking. "Or
is it just some front you feel you need to present to people?"

He grinned and took a swig of his wine, his eyes never
leaving mine. Maybe it was the coca leaf tea but despite the
couple of KOs he'd given me I wasn't afraid of him.

"That's for you to decide—if you've a mind to."

I wanted to look round for the nearest heavy object to
bash him with, pacifist as I am. But behind the cockiness it
was plain to see that self-loathing ran deep. I hadn't been in
therapy for nothing.

"On a scale of one to ten how much do you hate yourself?" I said. He drained his glass.

"Which is top of the scale—one or ten?"

He kept his eyes on me, then reached over and squeezed my bicep.

"Sorry, pal. I've never loved anyone like I loved Catherine. Find it difficult to deal with her having other men."

"Time you grew up then," I said, wanting desperately to rub my bicep. He had a strong grip.

There was something entirely vulnerable about him under the bluster and the aggression. I wasn't intending to forgive him for his treatment of other people, particularly women, but I was unexpectedly moved that he seemed so lost.

I was reminded of my earlier feelings about his death wish. And looking at the way he drained his glass and poured another almost in the same moment I saw not a man who was an alcoholic but a man who didn't really give a fuck, although maybe that came to the same thing.

He looked at me.

"There's something about you, Madrid, kind of gets under the skin. Makes a person want to tell you things."

"So tell me," I said.

"Do you know *Confessions of A Justified Sinner*?" he said, gripping my arm again.

"Sure, doesn't everybody," I said, wincing.

"I don't mean the album I mean the book."

"I mean the book, too."

The James Hogg book was one of my dark favorites, a Gothic story not of good and evil but of evil and evil—or more precisely how banality can be turned to evil uses. The plot, in case you don't know it, charts the descent into hell of a Calvinist young man whose belief in justification by faith is twisted by the Devil into a belief that any action he takes is justified. His actions include murdering his parents and his stepbrother.

The Devil goads him on in various guises but often the guise is that of the Calvinist himself. The Devil as *doppelganger* commits horrific crimes that the Calvinist has no memory of.

Aside from the fact the Devil must be pretty bored to spend so much time winning the soul of this oik, the book is very atmospheric, especially in its description of late eighteenth century Edinburgh. I wasn't surprised when it was made into a movie, but I had been surprised to discover Otis's interest in it.

"I've been betrayed by friends who led me into bad ways. You know I've been in hospitals, the psychiatric unit? The drink and the drugs. Lots of blank spaces.

"I've done things I don't remember doing. Even wondered if I had a *doppelganger*, like the Sinner, doing some of this stuff. But the psychiatrist explained it was just me refusing to take responsibility for the bad parts of me or the bad things I've done. That's where the Devil comes from, you know—people externalizing their own bad actions."

In my new post-therapy persona I was hip to the 'real meaning of things,' even if my therapist had been a con-person. Doppelganger—the double or shadow who gets the blame for your own bad actions—is classic delusionary stuff.

"You saying that when you get drunk you have memory lapses?"

"That would be a cop-out, wouldn't it? Something convenient for fiction writers. But with the drugs as well ..." He shrugged his big shoulders. "My memory is like Swiss cheese. It has all these big holes in it."

"You mean like the sixties—if you can remember them you weren't there?"

"Just blank spaces."

He drank his wine. After a few moments I said: "I was sorry to hear about your son."

His eyes filled with tears.

"Didn't think I could have kids, you see. One of the reasons Catherine and I didn't last—took it out on her."

"I think you're a real shit with this violence-to-women thing."

"You think I don't?" he said, his voice thickening. He balled his fists, held them in front of him. The swelling on the right one had gone down but the knuckles were still raw. I looked at the scars on the left one. He unclenched his fists and turned his hands palm up.

"I look at these fists that I've used to bludgeon and these fingers that I play my music with and I can't seem to put the two together." He chewed his moustached. "I don't know what to say to you. I loathe myself for how I abuse people. My music comes out of that loathing."

"That's your justification—other people's suffering allows you to create art?"

He wanted to get angry but his heart wasn't in it.

"I'm not trying to justify. I'm trying to explain something that torments me. The fact I push away those I most care about." He picked up his glass, held it loosely in front of him. "Except for my son and his mother. They were taken from me."

He looked at me. Forced a smile.

"But you had something you wanted to tell me."

"Not about the death threats—at least I don't think so. Those are a thing of the past now, I expect."

"You reckon?" he said, giving me an odd look. He topped up both our glasses then waited for me to speak. I took a breath then told him all I'd found out about Horace.

He didn't interrupt once and it was clear he believed me. When I'd finished, instead of the rage I'd expected there was only sorrow. He had slumped in his seat. His eyes were fixed on the table between us. When he looked up his eyes were full of tears again. He seemed such a little boy lost I wanted to hug him.

"Ah well," he said, his voice thick. "Ah well."

"I'm sorry," I said. "And to be the one to tell you."

"I think I knew. Just didn't want to face it. We met at a bad time for me. He helped me out of a hole. Got me back on my feet."

"You'd been pretty wild before then."

"As I said—some things I'm supposed to have done I can't believe I did. But yeah there are enough outrageous events for me to own up to."

"Is it true that in the early days you once turned a promoter upside down and shook your money out of him because he tried to run off without paying you?"

He smiled.

"They were always trying to rip you off in those days. If you were supposed to get a percentage of the bar they'd lie about the takings. If it was on the door they'd lie about how many people had come in, as if you couldn't count them for yourself on stage. First song I did I was always a bit distracted because I'd be counting heads."

He took a gulp of his wine.

"So this promoter?" I said helpfully.

"I'm sitting on stage in this church hall singing a song and suddenly see this promoter creep off down the center aisle. 'Stop him,' I shout, 'he's got my bleeding money.' Then I jump down off the stage and chase him. I catch him and I turn him upside down—he's only a little runt—and this roll of fives and ones and, Christ, ten bob notes in those days falls out of his jacket pocket.

"I'm tempted to take the lot for the aggro but I peel off what I'm owed and leave it at that. I don't want him to have an excuse to come back at me with the law, you know?"

He chuckled and shook his head.

"I was doing a gig in Washington once and I didn't know anybody. After a show I'm always pumped up. I went to this bar and had a few rounds and started feeling feisty so I gave the other guys at the bar the usual bollocks about Britain versus the States—I wasn't insulting or anything—well, not very—and the next thing I know the barman's laid a baseball bat across the side of my head. Out cold."

He sighed.

"I was bad those days."

"You're not bad now?"

"Too frigging old for that malarkey, mate. Being a yob is a young person's game. I take it easy now." He saw my look. "You were different pal. I've always been jealous." I continued to look. "The guy outside the club." He shook his head. "That's a blank space."

He'd finished the bottle. He looked at his watch.

"Got to do the soundcheck in half an hour."

"What will you do about Horace?"

"Sort him out after the concert. Do you think he could have been sending me death threats?"

"Not really. I think you have to distinguish between the people who send out death threats and the people who want you dead."

"Subtle distinction."

"Maybe. Maybe Benny sent you a death threat but I even doubt that. But don't sweat it. Now you're in Peru I'd be very surprised if you got any more threats."

"That right?" he said, getting to his feet. He reached into his jacket pocket and pulled out a folded sheet of paper. Dropped it on the table.

"Found it in my jacket pocket last night before I went on stage in Lima."

He stopped halfway to the door and looked back.

"Despite all the security whoever the bastard is was back-stage—in my dressing room."

"Wait—have you told Ralph?"

He carried on walking. Called back: "You tell him. Like I said—these bastards want me, they know where to find me. I don't give a shit any more."

I unfolded the paper. It was to the point. Someone had written out another couplet from Otis's hit "Sinner Man:"

*No power on earth can stop the Sinner Man*
*But the hellhound's on his trail*

Some people found the second line derivative of a Robert Johnson song title. Whatever. In this context the meaning seemed quite clear. Otis was still in danger.


I went for a walk around town. Aside from our trip to the Amazon, I had never felt more of an intruder into someone else's culture. Everywhere I looked were Indians living in poverty.

Essentially, I knew, they were Mongolian, as their flat cheek-bones and slightly slanted eyes showed. Around 20,000 B. C. Asian tribes had crossed the Bering Straits and drifted down through the Americas. There were many other tribes before the Incas came along. As Perry had pointed out, the Incas were in power for only a hundred years.

I reached the main square of the town, the Plaza de Armas, where tonight's concert would be held. A large stage jutted out from the steps below the cathedral. It was like a square in an old Spanish town, with enclosed wooden balconies hanging over it on three sides and arcades full of Indian market stalls.

It was big—some 5,000 people were expected to fill it in the evening. Every train and bus delivered another load of music-lovers, who were spread around the town since until this evening there was no access to the square.

The Square of War was only half the size of the original Inca square. When the Spanish arrived there was a stone covered in sheets of gold where offerings were made at the start of war.

Tupac Amaru, the last Inca emperor, was executed here—as, 300 years later, was Tupac Amaru II, the eighteenth century Indian leader who had led an uprising against the Spanish rulers.

The bearded Spanish conqueror Pizarro entered the city on 8 November 1533. He did no harm until the Emperor Manco escaped from imprisonment and returned with thousands of Indians for a six-month siege of the city.

On 6 May 1536 Manco launched his main attack, using slingshots to rain red-hot stones on the city. The city burned but the Spaniards survived the attack then set about pulling down the rest of the Inca buildings.

I looked around me at the impassive faces. Quite a few of the Indians were wearing brightly colored ponchos and blankets, the women wearing different sorts of round hats, papooses with babies in them on their backs.

According to my guide book there was a market down near the railway station. I made my way through twisting streets into a wide rectangle with stalls set out in three lines. I was standing in front of a stall that sold nothing but coca leaves when Bridget walked up to me.

"The elusive one," I said. I gestured round. "Isn't this great?"

"Terrific," she said. "Let's get a drink."

"I just want to haggle for some leaves," I said.

"Haggle? God, Nick, you're so mean. You're really bloody anal-retentive."

I clenched my buttocks as another salt-water induced spasm hit me.

"Anal-retentive sounds good to me just now," I said gloomily. "Anyway, they expect you to haggle—they get upset when you don't."

It took about ten minutes but I got the stallholder down to a sensible price.

"Well, I think I showed her," I said as we walked across the market to a bar on the corner.

"You certainly did," Bridget said, pointing at a sign in a shop window offering coca leaves at about half the price I'd paid.

We went up a steep flight of stairs to a first floor bar. It had a narrow wooden balcony—enough space for four tables open to the air and overlooking the square.

We squeezed either side of a table and sat down, ordering pisco sours. Bridget lit a cigarette and blew smoke over the next table.

I looked across at the stage. Otis was on stage with his band tuning up for the sound check. The cathedral rose behind it, the Andes behind that.

"Makes you want to be a condor, doesn't it?" I said. "Flying over these shingled roofs looking down on the square and the mountains all around it."

"You been at your coca leaf?" Bridget said. "I was reading about condors. I had it in my mind they were like eagles, these great predators soaring high among the mountaintops to the accompaniment of that poncy pipe music—I've seen the documentary, too."

"And your point is …" I said.

"My point is condors are vultures. They aren't like eagles at all. They don't hunt prey, they eat carrion—live off other people's leftovers. So much for noble fucking grandeur."

"You seem even more cynical than usual," I said. "Is this trip not working out as you expected?"

"It's had its moments," she said, watching Otis move around the stage. "How're things with you?"

"I told Otis about his manager. And he's had another death threat."

"You don't seem too concerned—nor him for that matter."

"I am but what can I do? Ralph's the man. And Otis doesn't seem too worried even though someone put this one in his jacket pocket. Backstage, that is. Which means either whoever is threatening Otis is incredibly devious or she or he's got contacts with the tour or—"

"He or she is on the tour."

"But who?" I said. "None of the obvious suspects seem to pan out."

"Except Horace."

"You really think it could be him? Otis said he was going to sort that situation out tonight. If that means an early bath for Horace then that should put an end to the nonsense."

"You think it is nonsense, then?" she said as the first chords of "Sinner Man" caroomed around the square.

"I can't really imagine Horace wanting to kill the goose that lays the golden egg."

"Unless exposed—in which case he might have to," Bridget said.

I heard what she said but I didn't respond. Our balcony was virtually on the corner of the square. Diagonally opposite was another larger, enclosed balcony, part of a restaurant. Sitting some twenty yards away from us on that balcony, in a bright Hawaiian shirt, was the guerrilla leader wanted by four South American countries. Our old friend Ferdinand Porras.

# THIRTEEN

"Wait here," I said to the astonished Bridget as I brushed past her and headed for the stairs. I was down the stairs and halfway across the street before I gave any thought about what I intended to do. Confront the guy, that was clear. But then what? I could hardly carry out a citizen's arrest. Especially as he was likely to be armed.

I needed a policeman. And whilst in Britain you can never find one when you need one, here in South America you couldn't walk ten yards without tripping over one, usually decked out in jackboots and spurs with a sabre dangling at his belt. I kid you not—whoever has the contract to make jackboots for South American security forces is on to a job for life.

So here was one preventing people going into the square, redirecting traffic to do a big detour around it. But if Porras was sitting here so openly he must be squared away with the local police.

I hovered in the street, unsure what to do. The policeman—middle height, portly, wearing mirror shades, and, yes, highly polished jackboots—had an arrogant bearing. If he were to move I just knew he would strut, although maybe that came with the jackboots.

Maybe I should get Ralph. I looked beyond the policeman and could see him on the edge of the stage. But even supposing

I could get into the square, by the time I reached Ralph and explained, Porras would have gone. I was dithering about what to do when Bridget came out of the bar.

"What the hell are you up to?" she demanded, stomping up to me. "How dare you leave me with the bill?"

"Bridget, this is hardly the time to discuss etiquette," I said fiercely. "I've just seen Ferdinand Porras." I gestured behind me. "Up in this restaurant. I was going to—"

Suddenly a waiter from the bar we'd left hurtled out into the street and rushed across to us brandishing a bill.

"You didn't pay the bill?" I said to Bridget, exasperated

The waiter grabbed my arm and started to speak in rapid Spanish. He was clearly on Bridget's side in this. The policeman watched us from behind his mirror shades.

I stuffed a handful of notes into the waiter's hand, of God knows what denomination. "Get to Ralph!" I yelled at Bridget and set off into the restaurant.

"Who do you think you're ordering around?" I heard her snarl as I disappeared inside.

I took the stairs to the restaurant two at a time. At least that was my intention but then I'd forgotten the altitude. I stopped on about step six and took a couple of minutes to get my breath. Puffing and wheezing I made my slow way up the rest of stairs.

Nobody paid me any attention as I strode through to the balcony. When I got there a waiter was clearing a table of the remnants of three meals. Porras was gone.

I leant out of the open window and looked around. There was no sign of the guerrilla leader. However, I saw Bridget just below me break free of the waiter, do a body-swerve, and dash past the policeman, then start legging it into the center of the square.

I had assumed she would sweet-talk her way past the policeman, given that he had a pistol strapped to his thigh. I knew from experience Bridget could move fast, and the policeman was hindered by his spurs. But just in case he decided to draw his gun and shoot her—and she'd be really pissed off at me if that happened—I called down what I thought was the word for murder in Spanish.

The policeman stopped in his tracks and looked up at the window. I yelled again. He looked back towards Bridget, who by now was in the center of the square and I hoped out of accurate range, then back up at the window. I called again and he hurried towards the restaurant entrance.

I looked round to find half a dozen puzzled waiters standing behind me. I smiled cheerily and walked past them, scanning the restaurant for the exit Porras must have used.

It was adjacent to the steps I had entered by. I went through a door and down another flight of steps. This one brought me out into one of the arcades that lined the square. Each side of it was filled with street traders, their goods laid out on multi-colored blankets. I looked to the right and saw Porras with three other men turn onto the next side of the square.

They were heading towards the cathedral. I turned down the arcade but was stopped abruptly by a gang of American tourists who were photographing a woman in traditional cos-tume—round hat, colorful blanket wrapped round her, papoose at her back, baby's head sticking out of it over her shoulder, llama beside her with two wicker panniers strapped across it.

Local Indians live a fairly self-sufficient life, thanks to their llamas. They drink their milk, make clothes from their wool, fires from their droppings—hey, it takes all sorts, buddy. But a few had realized there was easier money to be made by turning themselves into tourist attractions.

At all the popular tourist sites they posed against the most spectacular views to give them that extra color. Quite rightly they wanted paying for it, as you discovered once you'd taken your picture.

I brushed past the tourists and charged down the arcade. Thirty yards down I was stopped by a train of pack llamas. I was beginning to feel I was trapped in some ethnic computer game. The llamas made their unhurried way along, each one loosely tethered to the one in front.

Call me boorish but one dromedary is pretty much like another as far as I'm concerned. Since I'd had a bad encounter with a camel once in somebody's back garden in Edinburgh— don't ask, you really don't want to know—I wasn't about to mess with these.

As I waited for the llamas to pass, I witnessed a disgusting phenomenon which of course I relish telling you. The lead llama suddenly lifted its tail and urinated, while continuing on its slow way. As it did so the lama behind dipped its head and—yech— drank the urine. Then it too lifted its tail.

Considering they were all in line it seemed reasonable to assume that each day the llama owner gave water only to one llama, the one at the front. In the course of the day the water would progress slowly down the line. The llama at the back looked really pissed off.

When they had passed I jostled my way along the next arcade. I'd lost sight of Porras now. I reached the cathedral and climbed half a dozen steps. I craned my neck for a sight of him. He was nowhere to be seen.

I went in to the cathedral by the side entrance.

The cathedral was vast—we're talking Notre Dame here. Much of the interior was lost in gloom since the only light was through the stained glass windows and from thin tallow candles.

It looked to my non-Christian eyes as if it had been divided into cathedralettes. I could see half a dozen pulpits around the place, each with its own set of pews or rows of chairs before it. There were a few hundred people wandering the aisles, gazing up at big gloomy paintings of scenes from Jesus's life.

They had been painted by Indians under the tutelage of Jesuits. Instructed to paint Roman soldiers and centurions and never having seen any, the artists painted the Romans as Spanish soldiers. Local food stuffs also made an appearance. A painting of the Last Supper featured maize, fried bananas, and—the center-piece—roast guinea pig.

There was a heady smell of incense in the air. I passed an image known as the Lord of the Earthquake—twenty-six kilos of solid gold studded with precious stones. Then there was an enormous solid silver altar donated by the first archbishop, who came with Pisarro. Generous of him, though I wondered where he got the money from. Not.

I couldn't see Porras anywhere. A couple of tour parties converged in the aisle I was walking down so I turned off and started to make my way to the main exit into the square, thinking that was the best way to get to Bridget and Ralph backstage.

I was just thinking how solid the walls must be if Otis could perform his soundcheck outside and I could hear nothing inside when I saw Otis, Ralph, and Bridget standing in a huddle by the vast double doors leading onto the square. Ralph must have pulled Otis in there as soon as Bridget reached them.

I was walking along the back wall of the cathedral. Some twenty yards beyond Otis, Ralph, and Bridget I saw a big tour party following a woman wearing ethnic chic and holding an umbrella aloft.

In the gloom as I walked towards Otis and the others I caught a flash of scarlet among the dowdily dressed tourists. There was an attractive South American woman in a sleeveless red dress cut quite low at the front. She looked vaguely familiar. So did the dress.

I was musing on the fact that bare-armed women weren't usually allowed in Catholic churches in Europe when I realized I knew both dress and girl. It was Bridget's red dress, abandoned on the Amazon. And the girl who had been one half of our night guard was in it.

Startled, I watched her progress though the tourists. She had a cold look on her face. She was gaunt, her eyes luminous and large. Otis, Ralph, and Bridget were busy talking—or rather Bridget was talking at them.

I started to run.

I had about a hundred yards to cover, the woman in the red dress about fifteen. Another group of tourists debouched into the aisle in front of me. And stopped. The girl's handbag was slung round her neck. She was holding it to her belly with both hands. She walked decisively forward, her eyes fixed on the unsuspecting trio. So this was it.

But what exactly? What was she going to do? Shoot Otis? Was there a bomb in her handbag?

I didn't think Porras went in for suicide bombing. I recalled the girl's lover and looked round anxiously to see if he was approaching from another direction.

The cathedral was noisy, guides voices raised to describe its wonders. Echoing, refractive, a susurrus of sound. Someone started to play the organ, very loudly.

I called to Otis. People nearby turned and stared. My endangered trio remained oblivious. The tour party formed a solid wedge in front of me. I swerved to my right and jumped up onto a pew, ran along, feeling it wobble beneath me. I called their names again.

Everybody in the cathedral aside from the three people whose attention I was trying to attract seemed to be aware of my antics. Including the girl. She caught sight of me and blinked but didn't halt her progress. Rather the contrary. As I clattered along the pews she gave me a fierce look and reached into her handbag.

I was feeling pretty damned Douglas Fairbanks as I leapt from pew to pew, hearing each one topple over just as I moved on to the next. Once I was past the tourists I jumped back into the aisle. Theoretically.

My yoga-honed body was supposed to glide through the air then hit the ground running. But I caught my foot on the back of the last pew and went sprawling on the cold, very hard marble.

I scrabbled to my feet as people surged round me. Not to help me, you understand. They cast disapproving glances down at me but passed by. I looked wildly over to Otis. He was still talking to Ralph. I couldn't see Bridget. Nor the girl.

Jostled by the tour group I looked anxiously for a glimpse of the long black hair, the wounded eyes, the red dress. Then suddenly she was standing beside me. Frozen, I watched her fumble in her bag then bring out a gun. She pointed it at me.

"You killed my lover," she said huskily.

"Wha—"

"My red dress looks good on you," I heard a familiar voice say. The next thing I knew, Bridget had swung her handbag down and knocked the gun to the floor. I kicked it under the pew. Bridget clamped the girl's arms to her sides from behind. She's better at the rough stuff than me, as she's demonstrated on a number of occasions.

Then Ralph was beside us, speaking into the microphone jutting from his jaw.

"I was following Porras," I said quickly. "She's with him."

Four more security men burst through a small door inset into the larger door. Each hastily genuflected and made the sign of the cross before hurrying over.

Ralph hustled everybody out. Bridget and I hung back.

"I think she was going to shoot me." I was embarrassed to say words I'd only ever heard in movies. "Er—I think you saved my life."

"It's okay," she said abstractedly, looking after Otis. "I can't believe that guy."

"Who?"

"Otis—acts as if we never met." She shook her head and moved off. People were staring at me. Self-consciously I walked over and righted the pews I'd tipped. I quickly picked up the woman's gun, stuffed it into my knapsack, then followed the others out of the door.

Ralph and Bridget were standing with the girl in a portacabin behind the stage. Otis had been whisked back to the hotel. An unnecessary precaution since it turned out the girl wasn't after him. As she'd briefly indicated she was after me and Bridget.

"But why?"

"Your friends murdered my lover Danilo."

"No friends of mine," I said. "But wasn't he killed in a gun battle?"

"He was executed."

"How do you know?"

"I saw. I was hiding. He made me hide. Your friends disarmed him, made him kneel, then they shot him." She looked at the floor. "And I did nothing. I was a coward. But no longer."

I remembered Harry talking about the usual rules of engagement. I was also thinking of pat sayings like he who lives by the gun shall die by the gun.

"How old are you?" I asked.

"Eighteen," she said sullenly. "And Danilo was the same."

"I'm sorry about your friend, sister," Bridget said. "But you did kidnap us. Those guys were rescuing us. Danilo was armed—he would have shot us if we'd tried to escape."

"Danilo didn't even know how to shoot," she said. "He'd only been with us a couple of weeks."

"But he'd chosen that life—"

"You think we have options?" the guerrilla girl said, her eyes flashing. "We have no options at all. Danilo came from a village just outside Bogota, my country's capitol. His family worked in the coal mines. You know about our coal mines?" She bared her teeth in a cold grin.

"They profit from child slavery—10,000 child miners work in these coal mine—they work the seams that are too small for adults, in unsupported tunnels, without gas extraction, working by candlelight. It is a short life for most of them. Explosions are common. Danilo's two brothers were both cripples—one lost his legs when they were amputated by a runaway coal wagon, the other has a terrible lung disease. Danilo left before the mines claimed him.

"Colombia is rich in minerals, you know—precious metals, base metals, and gemstones. It is the world's leading producer of emeralds—before the drug barons, the emerald miners divided the country into private fiefdoms. They too have used child labor to accumulate vast wealth, but none of that wealth comes to us.

"My family is from one of the indigenous tribes. The U'Wa. You may have read that 6,000 U'Wa Indians have threatened to commit suicide if Occidental Petroleum continues its oil explorations on our land." She curled her lip. "Suicide is not my way. If I die it will be with a gun in my hand."

"Who killed Joel?" I said.

"I don't know. Perhaps Ferdinand, perhaps your friends."

"You're here with Porras?" I said.

She shook her head.

"Come on—I saw him not five minutes before I saw you."

She looked puzzled.

"Ferdinand here?"

Did she really not know?

"Damned right lady," Ralph said. "And we need to know what he's after. Is he going to kill Otis or kidnap him?"

"I have no idea. I have not seen him since I left Leticia. I flew here and I waited for you to arrive—I heard you speak of this concert tour."

I drew Ralph away.

"What do you think?"

"I think we cancel the concert, except Otis and Horace won't hear of it."

"You've spoken to them together?"

"Separately. Why?"

"I told Otis about Horace."

Ralph nodded slowly.

"Ah."

"I believe her about Porras by the way," I said.

"Me too. What do you want me to do with her?"

"Me?"

"It's you and Bridget she tried to kill. May still want to kill. Up to you to press charges."

I pondered for a moment.

"What're the cops like in Peru?"

Ralph scarcely raised his eyebrow.

"They'd brutalize her, wouldn't they?"

"Would you ask that if she was an ugly guy?"

"I hope so. Would they?"

"At least that, yes."

"Kill her?"

"Probably."

"Can we let her go?"

"What if she comes after you again?"

"Can I talk to her alone?"

When I went back in she was sitting very upright at the table, bizarrely glamorous in her red dress. She didn't look at me as I sat down.

"We're going to let you go," I said.

She looked puzzled.

"Why?"

"I don't want to see you come to any harm."

"I should be grateful?"

"Only grateful enough not to kill Bridget or me. You know we had nothing to do with Danilo's death. We didn't know the people who rescued us. We didn't ask to be kidnapped."

Her eyes were solemn.

"I became a guerrilla for political reasons. I didn't realize Ferdinand only wanted money until that conversation I heard him have with you. It disgusted me. Also, I hated Porras for his cruelty. His barbarism. He would gouge out people's eyes and chop their hands off. I heard that he once flayed all the skin off one soldier and left him to die in the village square in the midday sun."

She stood.

"May I go now?"

"Sure," I said.

"Can I have my gun back?"

I took it from my knapsack. It seemed somehow heavier. I put it on the table and pushed it across to her. She took it, expertly checked it, and stuck it in her bag.

"What will you do?" I said.

She shrugged then turned.

"Watch out for Ferdinand," she said. "He is ruthless." She moved to the door. Stopped again. "One more thing. He wouldn't alert a victim with threats. He would just get on with the job."


"You said she could go?" Bridget screeched. I thought I heard alarmed condors leave their nests atop remote Andean peaks.

I closed the open windows and turned to face her.

"She tried to kill you—us—you may recall. She would have killed you if not for me. She blames us for the death of her lover. And you said she could go."

"They'd have killed her, Bridget."

"Rather her than me."

Bridget ranted for ten minutes more but finally ran out of steam. A thought struck her.

"What happened to her gun?"

"I picked it up in the church."

"Really? Let me see it—I've never seen a gun close up."

"I—er—gave it back to her."


When I could walk again I thought I'd kill the time before the concert in a bar with a pisco sour or two. I found one that seemed full to bursting with backpackers from the U. S. and Europe. It was incredibly noisy—loud conversation and a band in the corner playing electro-Andean music.

I noticed people glancing over occasionally to a dark corner of the bar where a man in shades was sitting, a bottle of wine at his side. The Late Great Otis Barnes, a little the worse for wear.

"Otis?" I said, standing over him for a change.

He looked in my direction. Nodded. I wondered what concoction he'd been frying his brains with today.

"How's it going?"

"Okay," he said.

I jerked a thumb over at the musicians.

"You going to be dancing again?"

"It takes two to tango," he said.

"Salsa, you mean."

He shook his head.

"Whatever."

"Bit of excitement earlier."

He nodded slowly. I could see this was going to be hard work.

"Have you spoken to Horace?" I said.

He looked at me for a long moment then shook his head. The waiter brought my drink and I sat there wondering what to do. I glanced to either side but I couldn't see his bodyguards. Had he slipped the leash? He leaned forward.

"Bet you had a happy childhood," he said.

"Not particularly," I said.

"I was in and out of mental homes when I was a kid," Otis said.

"I didn't know that," I said. Which wasn't very exciting I know but you have to kind of edge into these things—trust me, I'm a journalist.

"Why would you?" he said. "I never told nobody before."

I was intrigued by the way that under stress he lapsed into some primordial cockney accent, the Sarf London patois favored by all rock stars of his generation who wanted to keep their street cred.

"I kept hearing voices, see, telling me to do things. Bad things. They said I skinned my cat once. You know that saying? About skinning a cat? They find this cat at the bottom of our back garden, hanging from a tree, skinned.

"They said it was my cat and I'd done it. I asked them how they knew it was my cat—I mean a lump of meat hardly has any identifying features does it? And its collar and nametag were gone. My dad just beat me worse."

I stared hard.

"And had you?"

"Skinned my cat? I loved that cat. I'd had it since it were a kitten. Gimme some credit, please. What kind of sicko do you think I was?"

Otis looked away and then back.

"It was the neighbor's cat I'd skinned. Just out of scientific curiosity, you understand. And it didn't suffer—I bashed it with a big stone first.

"But when our cat came home safe and sound did I get an apology? Did I hell. You know what my dad did as punishment? He drowned my cat. Where's the fucking logic in that, eh? Where's the fucking logic?"

"Does seem a bit hard on the cat," I agreed, feeling queasy. I'm quite soppy about cats actually. This was a side of Otis I'd never seen and I wasn't sure I wanted to.

I'd always assumed his violence was impulsive, born out of anger, but now I wondered if there was something colder, more sadistic about it. Of course, the story he'd recounted went back to his childhood—I assumed he'd had treatment since. Been cured.

"So you had treatment?" I said. "In the mental hospital."

"Well, they put me away, if that's what you mean. After, you know, my mum and dad."

"Your mum and dad?"

"Classic Oedipal complex the bloke in the white coat said."

"How classic?" I said with a nervous smile.

"Very classic," he said, his mouth turned down.

I knew about the Oedipus complex. You engage in rivalry with your father for love of your mother. Your father tries to castrate you to stop you but you kill him instead. You're two years old. Clearly absurd but if any of my younger readers should see their fathers coming towards them with a meat cleaver, toddle like hell.

"That would be … er …" I said.

"That would be screwing my mother and killing my father."

I looked at him intently. It suddenly seemed very quiet in the bar, although the noise hadn't noticeably lessened.

"Are you saying you did these things, or are you speaking metaphorically?"

"I did worse. Mum died, too. Worst case of arson the police had ever seen. Well, if you're going to do a job, do it properly, eh?"

He looked at me quite calmly.

"Now you know a big secret about me. How can I be sure you won't tell anyone else?"

"No, no, your secret's safe with me. You've paid your debt to society … er, you have, haven't you?"

He grinned a weird grin.

There was a reception shortly organized by the town council for the rock tour. I wasn't sure Otis was in a fit state to attend.

"I'm going to go back to the hotel, get spruced up to meet the mayor," I said, trying to hide my disgust. "You coming?"

"Be along," he said.

I looked back as I was leaving the bar. He still had the weird grin on his face. He raised his hand in a small wave.

Ralph was the first person I saw at the hotel.

"No word on Porras yet," he said. "I've told all the local and government authorities—they'll be rousting the usual suspects around here. We've got Otis pretty well covered as a kidnap risk but if Porras had anything more in mind—well, there's not much anybody can do against a sniper with a high-powered rifle except not go on stage. And Otis, as you know, is determined to go on."

"This covering of Otis—your security guards work deep, do they?"

"In what sense?"

"The ones guarding Otis—like you wouldn't know they were there?"

He frowned.

"I guess. What's your point?"

"I just left him in a bar over near the square and I didn't spot a soul keeping an eye on him."

"Damn that man." He clicked on his radio. "Raoul? Where the hell are you and where is Otis?" Ralph listened then relaxed his shoulders. "A bar? Okay."

He looked at me. "Everything is copasetic. Otis just came into the hotel through the back entrance. His guys were sitting in another part of the bar keeping an eye out—guess you didn't spot them."

"That's a relief," I said. "So what about Porras? Which way do you think he's going to jump?"

"Porras is a hard-ass. Don't let that charming smile fool you. The bad guys in Colombia are a whole other breed when it comes to cruelty."

"So the guerrilla girl indicated," I said.

Ralph saw my expression.

"Colombia has a long history of torture and cruelty. They had a civil war back in 1948—La Violenca it was called. Men were castrated, had their *cojones* stuffed in their mouths. Both sides decapitated their enemies and used their heads as footballs in the village squares.

"People were thrown out of airplanes or over cliffs or were burned alive. For women it was even worse. Rape was the least of it."

One way and another I was in a very subdued mood when I left Ralph. The things Otis had told me about himself had horrified me. The things Ralph had told me about Porras had shaken me even further.

My mood didn't lift at the reception. Bridget flirted shamelessly with the mayor's male secretary. The rock stars were on their best behavior, though God knows what these very straight, formal Peruvian officials thought of their dress sense—even the security guards were dressed better than the musicians.

Otis was here with Conchita, and whilst I could see tension in his face and in the way he held himself, he seemed a lot better than he had earlier. I wasn't sure how he'd feel about having told me his childhood secrets but when he first saw me he gave me a cheery wave. I didn't respond.

Horace was there for a time in a white linen suit and black floral waistcoat—someone should really have a word with this guy. I saw him with Otis talking to the mayor and Otis looked across at me, a taut expression on his face.

This evening's concert and the climactic concert on top of Machu Picchu were being filmed for worldwide TV and video sales. The film crew was allowed a certain amount of backstage access and also had a camera at this reception. To avoid it I walked over to the window.

The scene was magical. The sun was fading, casting a pink glow over the square and cathedral. Tiers of whitewashed buildings with red-tiled roofs stretched away up the hills on every side. Balconies painted blue were illuminated by the soft yellow light of elegant lamps fixed to the walls.

The square was already full of people sitting on the floor listening to some Andean pipe music. People were crammed onto each of the balconies overlooking them.

Those of us not performing were invited to stay here and watch the concert. I couldn't see Bridget for the moment. As I looked around Perry caught my eye.

"Dig this place man. Dig this place. Those Incas were really something."

"This is mostly Spanish you're seeing here."

"Sure but those central gutters down the center of the streets—Inca. Used to keep them filled with rushing water from the mountains to keep the city clean. You know they built this city in the shape of a puma?"

"I didn't know that. Why?"

"Damned if I know but it's a fact. Their capitol. Their empire stretched from the Ecuador/Colombia border to the Rio Maule in southern Chile. You got the Amazon jungle in the east, the Pacific coast in the west."

"I know. What's your point Perry?"

"Treasure. You know gangs of *huaqueros*—treasure hunters—plunder sites all over Peru. There are too many sites to be policed or protected by archaeologists. They're finding new ruins all the time—in the forests around Machu Picchu for example. Then there's the legendary lost city of Paititi—people search for it every year without success."

"What's your point?"

"A freebooter like myself could find a fortune here. I'm thinking of staying on like my great-grandfather."

"Your great-grandfather?" Bridget said, appearing from nowhere and leaning against me.

Perry looked from one to the other of us.

"This reminds me of him."

"Who're you talking about?" I said.

"Who the hell do you think? Harry Alonzo Longabaugh and Robert Le Roy Parker—with Etta Place of course," he said, nodding to Bridget.

"Of course," I said, glancing back at the square.

"Butch and Sundance!" Perry declared intently.

"Oh yeah—good film. 'Swim? The fall will probably kill you.'" He grimaced.

"The movies?" he spat. "I'm talking about the real thing. I'm their descendant."

"Both of them?" I said, puzzled.

"They were an item," Bridget said. "You've only got to see the movie to see that."

"Longabaugh—Sundance—and Etta?" I said.

"Parker—Butch—and a local girl in Argentina."

"I thought they went to Bolivia?" I said. "When I say Bolivia you just think California. You just keep thinking Butch, that's what you're good at."

"Do you ever listen to yourself?" Bridget said, gazing at me blankly.

"Harry and Etta left for Argentina 1901, were joined by Robert Le Roy Parker in 1902," Perry recited. "Ranched until 1905 then in 1906 turned up in Bolivia via Chile. Worked for Percy Siebert at the Concordia tin mine from the end of 1906 to sometime in 1908. Held up the Aramayo payroll in early November—then there was the famous shoot-out in San Vicente in southern Bolivia a few days later on 6 November 1908. Butch and Sundance were undoubtedly involved but—" he leaned towards us, "—there's no proof they were killed."

We both looked at him for a moment. His eyes were bulging a little. Finally Bridget said: "So *they* killed Kennedy."

Perry drew back.

"What's your point, Perry," I said in irritation.

"He has no point. He never has a point."

Perry looked at Bridget.

"How can you say that? We've only just met. Usually it takes people a couple of weeks to find that out."

"I'm a quick study," Bridget said shortly.

"Actually I do have a point. My point is it's all disguises down here. A person can come here and reinvent himself, be who he wants to be."

"Is that what you want to do?" Bridget said.

"Doesn't everybody?" he said.

"I've always had a vague wish to be Marlene Dietrich," Bridget murmured. "Nick has too for that matter."

"Ha ha," I said, wondering when I'd ever let that slip.

Bridget took my arm and led me away.

"I'm forgiven then?" I said. "For letting the girl go?"

"You know me—I forgive easily. I just never forget."

"Where are you taking me?"

"Don't raise your hopes—just to see the concert, but I need to nip back to the hotel and I'm not going anywhere without you whilst Annie Oakley is out there somewhere."

As we came down the steep street to our hotel entrance I was surprised to see Otis and Horace standing at the entrance to an alleyway beyond the hotel. Horace had a puzzled look on his face. It seemed a curious time for Otis to be bearding him.

I watched as Otis put his big arm round Horace's narrow shoulders and drew him into the alley. It was the last time I saw Horace alive.

# FOURTEEN

When Horace didn't show for the train to Machu Picchu next day I thought Otis must have fired him. The concert had gone off without a hitch. Otis and Conchita had been in fine form and at the end had duetted on four numbers: two of her hits in which Otis got a roar of approval for singing in Spanish, followed by two of his, including a sinuous version of "Sinner Man" in which Conchita came down heavy on being the hellhound on his trail.

There was a party afterwards but I was tired and we had an early start the next morning for Machu Picchu. The government had offered a helicopter but Otis suggested everybody take the spectacular train journey.

The train left at six and even Bridget was up in time, although she went to sleep as soon as she boarded it and remained so until it had completed its three-hour journey.

We were travelling in a special carriage on the daily tourist train—an old diesel in colorful red and yellow livery. Another carriage had been loaded with the equipment in the course of the night. Men with rifles were guarding it and us.

It was a chilly morning and the station was a colorful bustle of tourists, backpackers, Indian vendors, hawkers, and thieves. (Actually, I'm not sure whether there were any hawkers there—I don't really know what they do—but it sounds right.)

Had the train been a steam engine belching out plumes of steam it would have been perfect. As it was the diesel coughed up greasy black smoke, which wasn't quite the same.

Our carriage was packed with goodies and a few people hit the beers, which at that time of the morning showed remarkable commitment.

The train's first challenge was to leave Cusco. It did this in fits and starts, a hundred yards forwards, fifty yards back, zigzagging up a steep series of switchbacks to emerge, eventually, on the high plains of the Andes.

An hour into the journey Richard came over to me.

"Otis wants a word."

"What's up?"

"Dunno. He'll only tell you."

Still unable to forget the awful thing Otis had told me about killing his parents, I approached him cautiously. I really didn't much care for him any more.

"Madrid, just the man. Thanks Rick, you can leave us together."

He handed me a beer. It was nine o-clock by now. Still too early for me, but what the hell?

We were running alongside the Urubamba River, which flowed down from the high valleys to the Upper Amazon then down to the real thing. It almost felt like Bridget and I were coming full circle.

"Did you have your talk with Horace?" I said, looking for a reaction.

"Bastard must have got wind that I knew. I was going to talk to him after the gig but I couldn't find him. Hadn't checked out of his room this morning. Probably skulking somewhere until we've moved on then he'll run back home."

"I thought you might have had a chat with him earlier," I said hesitantly.

"At the reception? That would have been timely—I don't think."

"And you didn't see him after that?"

"I thought I just said that. Didn't I just say that? Anyway, Horace isn't why I wanted to talk to you."

"But aren't you worried he'll be ripping you off even as we speak?"

"No chance. I phoned through to my London office, got a block put on everything as soon as you told me about all this. Maybe that's how he guessed the game was up."

He reached into his pocket, pulled out another folded sheet of paper.

"I got another one of these last night. And this one was in my frigging bedroom. Waiting for me when I got back after the gig."

He took a swig of his beer. "Whoever is doing this is really pissing me off."

As best I could remember it was the same handwriting as before. It was the last two lines of "Sinner Man," when the Devil as the Sinner's doppelganger finally catches up with him.

*And when you finally face yourself*
*Which of you comes out alive?*

I looked at it blankly for a moment. What was occupying my thoughts was the fact that Otis had denied seeing Horace after the reception, yet I'd seen them together with my own eyes. I had a sudden, horrible thought. Otis was sending the death threats to himself.

"How could someone get into your bedroom?"

"That's what I wondered and then I thought they'd probably bribed the chambermaid to leave it there. But I guess the how is less important that the what. Clearly I'm about to get my comeuppance."

"At the concert at Macchu Picchu?"

"I guess so."

He looked at his big hands. Flexed them. "Well, we've all got to pay for our sins sometime. I'm definitely overdue."

Ralph had gone ahead by helicopter to Machu Picchu to sort out security. Presumably that was why Otis had spoken to me instead.

"What are you going to do?" I said.

"Keep on keeping on," he said with a shrug.

Conchita came over a few moments later so I excused myself and went back to my seat.

I was thinking that I only had Otis's word for the last two messages. The very first had been written on his hotel's stationery in Bogota. I pondered his mental health. When I heard two hours later that Horace's dead body had been found down an alley near our Cusco hotel, I pondered even more.

Our train journey took us from the high plains down through gorges so narrow you could reach out of the window and touch the sheer rockface, then on into tropical forest known locally as the "eyebrow of the jungle."

The train finally stopped at a place called Aguas Calientes, named after some dubious hot springs.

"What'd I tell you?" Perry said. "Butch and Sundance country right here."

Aguas Calientes was indeed like a frontier town, a one-horse town without the horse though with runty pigs wandering down the main street. The only street actually, running either side of the railway line. It was full of cheap restaurants and tacky tourist shops.

The river was a series of foaming rapids here, tumbling over hidden rocks, a sheer cliff face on the far bank towering over it, the water booming as it rushed so you had to shout to make yourself heard. All around us high green peaks with one of them shrouded in cloud, a blue sky above. And somewhere hidden above on a rocky spur was the holy Inca place, Machu Picchu.

Ralph was on the platform with a dozen men when we pulled in. He looked very solemn. He took Otis to one side. Watching through the train windows I saw Otis slump, lowering his head and shaking it slowly.

Bridget stirred.

"Have I missed much?" she said, yawning.

"Five hundred years of history, but apart from that, no."

She looked out of the window, took in the ramshackle shop front.

"I assume you booked the first-class hotel through the same agent you used for the Amazon one," she said, deadpan.

Actually Richard had booked us all into some sumptuous place here in town—where it could be hiding, I didn't know.

We got off the train to see Otis and Ralph walking away down the line. A solemn-faced Richard waited for us to tell us Horace was dead.

"Battered to death in an alley just across from the hotel."

"A robbery?" I said, though I felt sure of the answer.

"His credit cards and wallet had gone but he'd lain there all night so someone could have rolled him after death."

Bridget grimaced. I felt nauseous. I recalled the beating Otis had given to the man outside the club in Bogota.

Richard led us down the platform onto the railway line.

"Ralph thinks it's linked to the threats—he's doubled the security on Otis."

I was remembering Otis's weirdness, almost a lethargy when we talked in the bar. He definitely seemed to be on the brink of something. And if he could kill his own parents ...

But what was he intending to do? Was he aiming to kill himself? Would that end the death threats for good?

The problem with suicidal nutters—excuse the technical

term, it's all the therapy I've been doing—is they like to take other people with them.

We left the town and continued to walk along the track between breeze-block shanty houses, most with no roof, some with a wall or two missing. Half a dozen pigs rooted among garbage. Some ten yards to our right and maybe twenty feet below us the Urubamba roared and boomed.

"Whoa, Richard," Bridget said. "This is the way to a five-star hotel? I've been this way before with dickhead here."

"Trust me, I'm in PR," Richard said reflexively. "Thing is, I didn't like Horace much—who did?—and then you told me, Nick, that he was ripping Otis off—hey, this is bad news for Otis isn't it?"

"How do you figure that?" I said, stepping out of the way of a small black pig intent on keeping me company. It was quite cute, actually, but my mind was on what I should do about Otis.

"Horace is dead before Otis could sue his ass to get his money back."

"He can sue the estate," Bridget said, stopping abruptly before a large pool of some unidentified liquid. She looked back.

"Where's our luggage?"

"They're going to shunt the carriage back down the line to the hotel and offload everything."

I was only half-listening. Puzzling over what to do I therefore only half-heard the words "President's wife."

"Say what about the President's wife?"

"It won't affect her visit tonight."

"The President's wife is coming tonight?" I said, stopping in my tracks—well, track.

"Where is this fucking hotel, Richard," Bridget shouted as she turned her ankle yet again. Four-inch heels weren't perhaps the best footwear for this kind of terrain.

"There," Richard said, pointing off to our left. And there,

sure enough was a smart hotel sign and a flagged path leading up through the exotic foliage of hibiscus, bougainvillea, and big yuccas.

"She's flying in by helicopter just before the concert starts. She'll open the event then fly out again. Be gone in thirty minutes. They'll pretend she's staying for the concert but of course she won't."

The hotel was a series of white-painted, timber roofed bungalows set among the jungle trees and bushes. It was the kind of hotel our hotel in the Amazon aspired to be one day—rough-edged enough to make you think you were roughing it but with constant running water and a mini-bar in each room.

The hotel's main building was expensively primitive—tiled floors, wooden roof, great slabs of wood for tables. The bar and restaurant both looked out over the Urubamba River rushing pell-mell below.

I went to my bungalow and lay on the bed. I needed to tell Ralph about Otis and Horace, but first I had to find him. Bridget came with me to Machu Picchu by bus. The site was already closed to the public in preparation for the concert.

"Is Ralph inside?" I asked Raoul, who was on guard at the entrance gate. He nodded.

"And Otis?"

He nodded again.

I walked in—slowly, because it was steep. Machu Picchu was quite a sight. The collection of ruined buildings took up relatively little space. The ruins, perched above deep gorges, included majestic staircases, temples, palaces, towers, fountains, and a sundial.

Several higher peaks towered over it, the closest of which was Huayc Pichu right beside it.

There was one large stage but also a series of smaller stagings in different parts of the site. The concert was going to be an ambitious *son et lumiere* display. Light-cannons would project an alphabet of universal human symbols—recognizable and pleasing shapes—across the mountains.

The light-cannons were giant projectors that cast light over an area of 10,000 square meters at a distance of up to a kilometer. They were on the hills around—one was up on Huayc Picchu.

We wandered across the site—carefully, for breath had to be conserved. It was easy to forget down at Aguas Calientes that whilst you might be in a deep valley, the valley itself was already high in the mountains.

I saw the Joe Blows and Fertile Lands gathered over by the sacred altar. We walked over to join them.

"Hi," Catherine said, walking across to us. "We're fighting over who gets to play where. Everybody wants to be here—the backdrop down to the river valley is fantastic when they shoot from up there—" She pointed up behind us to what was known as the sacristy. The stage would be in front of the "hitching post of the sun," a tall slab of stone.

Modern archaeologists refer to them as gnomons—a vertical column that every Inca center had and which was used for astronomical observation and to calculate the passing seasons.

Catherine shrugged.

"Otis will be here, I guess." She pointed behind her across the wide grassy plaza below. There was a large rock there, the Sacred Rock, shaped to match the mountain skyline behind it. "We'll be over there—what a place to play, eh?"

"Have you seen Otis?" I said, rather more abruptly than I intended.

"Didn't know he was here yet," she said.

"Ralph?" I said.

"He's in a huddle somewhere with some government people."

She was watching my expression.

"Is there a problem you should share with the group? Some of us are feeling it's become a bit us-and-them around here."

"Can you spare ten minutes?" I said.

Catherine led the way back into the main plaza.

"Did Otis ever tell you about his childhood?" I said.

"Of course. And pretty brutal it was, too. His father sounds a nightmare."

"Did he tell you about the arson attack?"

"Arson? No."

"The mental homes?"

Catherine stopped.

"No."

"Otis told me he killed his parents either by or before setting fire to their house."

Catherine looked bewildered. Bridget looked as if she wanted to speak but felt she shouldn't—a first for her.

"He must have been having you on."

"I don't think so."

"Some strange joke—how drunk was he?"

"Hard to say. He was acting peculiarly."

Bridget was bursting to speak.

"He used to get pretty weird with the drugs."

"It sounded like a confession."

"But it can't be," Catherine said.

"Why?"

"Well, for one thing his mother is still alive. He bought her a bungalow in St. Annes. I've visited here there, for goodness' sake."

"His father?"

"He buggered off years ago. Died in a pub brawl in Doncaster. Otis went to the funeral."

I pondered this, then looked at Bridget, who could hold herself in no longer.

"He's been peculiar with me. Really friendly at first then cutting me dead then being friendly again."

"That's the drink," Catherine said.

"Do you think he's having a breakdown?" I said.

Catherine shrugged again.

"Sounds like."

I was relived that Otis hadn't done the terrible thing he'd claimed but I was worried by the state of mind of a man who would make up such a story. Then another thought began to form.

I decided not to tell them about seeing Otis with Horace.

"And you've not seen Otis here?"

"I didn't know he'd arrived," Catherine said again.

I looked round.

"He's here somewhere. I can't see Conchita either. Maybe he's with her."

"Probably," Catherine said, rather tartly. "But if you still want Ralph, last I saw of him he was up at the watchman's hut." She pointed to a terraced hill that rose behind the main complex of buildings to the west. At the top of a dog-leg flight of stairs there was a stone hut with a recently thatched roof. Bridget and I set off over there. I was about to share my new thoughts with her when she said: "So you think Otis is two verses short of a song?"

"Maybe. It's a shame, I kind of like him.

"Me too. Those shoulders. Lousy in bed though—drinks too much."

"Where did you hear that tittle-tattle," I said, puffing slightly as we started up the wide staircase.

"What—you hadn't noticed he drank too much? Haven't you seen the tankers pulling up outside whatever hotel he happens to be in?"

"I mean about being lousy in bed."

"Oh that." She paused to catch her breath, unusual color in her face. "Around," she said vaguely.

"Bridget you haven't? You *have*. When, for God's sake— you've only been with the tour three days and he's scarcely been out of Conchita's sight."

"Just long enough, honey."

She resumed the steps at a fast pace. I lagged behind, struggling for breath.

When we reached the top of the steps the hut was on a final spur of rock some twenty yards above.

"I was thinking Otis may have killed Horace," I said when I'd caught my breath. "Horace was ripping Otis off big time. I told Otis—"

"You told Otis?" she said. "You have been a busy bee."

"I saw him with Horace last night in the entrance to an alley about ten yards below the hotel. I saw Otis take him in the alley."

"The alley where he was found."

"Presumably, but that doesn't matter. On the train he told me he hadn't seen Horace at all last night. That's what I need to talk to Ralph about."

Bridget was looking back down to the entrance gate.

"Wrong place, wrong time, pardner."

I followed her glance. Ralph was standing by the covered entrance in conversation with someone hidden under the roofing. When the person stepped out, putting something in his pocket, I could see it was Otis.

"Double that," I said, adding absently: "We must have missed him going back out when we came in." I looked around then at the little map of the Machu Picchu site. "I'm not going to slog back down there now when we've only just got here. There's an Inca Bridge just down the trail here worth looking out for."

"That's your idea of a good time is it?"

"Well, yes, actually."

She led the way up past the so-called watchman's hut. The trail to the Inca Bridge was signposted due south.

"So you think Otis did for Horacce in Cusco?"

"It looks like it. He had a good motive and I did see them together."

"How was Otis when you told him about Horace's perfidy?"

"Perfidy?"

"Perfectly good word."

"That's why I'm surprised you're using it. He was subdued. As if it was just one more disappointment, one more person who had let him down."

The trail wound along the west flank of the mountain, among trees and shrubbery. To our right we had a staggering view of the Urubamba River curling through the valley far below.

As we turned the next bend Bridget suddenly drew me back.

"Perry"'s up ahead. One more daft conversation with him and I swear I'll throw him off this mountain."

I peeped round the corner. Perry was standing motionless in jeans and T-shirt. God knows how his winklepickers were coping with the narrow trail. He was sideways on to us and I could see he had a pair of binoculars trained off to our left.

"Let him go on ahead," Bridget whispered.

So we waited a few minutes until, apparently satisfied, Perry let the binoculars drop to his chest, and, looking quickly around him, set off along the trail.

We followed some fifty yards behind.

"Has Otis travelled with everyone else during the tour?" Bridget said as the trail grew narrower.

"Why?"

"I saw him in Bogota," Bridget said.

"I know," I said puzzled.

"I mean before the press conference."

"You couldn't have," I said. "He was on tour."

She shrugged.

"He must have flown in early."

I pondered for a moment. I do sometimes.

"Bridget, when exactly did you and Otis, er …"

"Shag?"

"If you will."

"After the Lima concert."

"You were together all night?"

"Be a bit frustrating, wouldn't it? He's a rock musician. Get an hour out of 'em if you're lucky." She grimaced. "I wasn't lucky. But why the prurient interest in my sex life?"

"Nothing," I mumbled, my brain working fast.

We turned the next bend and saw Perry twenty yards ahead fiddling with his shoe. We heard him curse.

"Godamn these fucking mountains."

Bridget and I skulked like naughty schoolchildren.

"Otis is in good, Nick, don't you think, considering his lifestyle over the years," Bridget murmured whilst we were waiting for Perry to go on ahead.

"He's been working out, that's for sure."

"But no double chin, no bags under the eyes. At fifty that's remarkable don't you think?"

Perry moved on and so did we. The trail had narrowed so much we could only walk in single file. We had the side of the mountain to our left and to our right a precipitous drop down the slope.

"You mean he's had a face job?" I said, trying not to slither as the trail sloped drastically. "Well, I know from personal experience Conchita has had a chest job—lay your head upon my breast but bring a pillow."

"You intrigue me," she said, just as I pulled to an abrupt halt. We had reached the beginning of a horseshoe bend. I could see Perry some forty yards ahead of me by the track, fifteen yards across a yawning gap that fell away to the river so far below.

He was approaching the Inca bridge. Here the trail was so narrow it was cut into the side of a sheer precipice. And just ahead of him the Incas had been obliged to build a vast buttress of dressed stone to provide a ledge for the path. A sheer wall of rock above, the Urubamba River so far below.

Perry, balancing with his left forearm against the sheer rock face, was making his careful way along the ledge towards the Inca bridge.

The bridge was little more than a gap in the buttress with two wooden logs laid across it. During Inca times, the Incas would simply withdraw the logs to make this part of the trail impassable.

The logs were across the gap now. Perry approached them hesitantly. He stopped when he reached them. Bridget slithered down behind me.

"Let's wait a minute," I said. "I can't figure out what Perry's up to."

Perry appeared to be waiting for something. Or someone. As he waited he looked nervously down at the precipitous drop to his right. Only once. He quickly drew back.

I could almost see him take a deep breath then shuffle out onto the logs, testing them for weight step by step. They held and he virtually ran the remaining five yards to the other side of the bridge.

"We're not supposed to go beyond the bridge," I murmured to Bridget. "Where's he going?"

As I said this I looked off to the right where the track continued. Six men in single file appeared on the bend. Perry had his attention focused on his feet as he moved slowly along the path. With every step he seemed to get more fearful.

However, my attention was focused on the figure at the head of the queue of men.

I was aware of Bridget at my side.

"Ferdinand Porras," she said.

# FIFTEEN

My first impulse was to call a warning across the gorge to Perry. But even I'm not that much of a fool. Walking down the track had been reasonably easy. Running back up at this altitude would be impossible.

A moment later I was glad I hadn't. Perry and Porras obviously knew each other. It had taken me a moment to recognize Porras since he was in fatigues rather than his trademark Hawaiian shirt, but there was no mistaking the moustache and the swept back hair.

"I was meeting you round the bend," Porras said. "Not here in full view of anyone who comes by."

Two men moved past Perry and headed along the trail towards us. Bridget and I looked at each other and shrank into the undergrowth.

"Now tell me—what the fuck is going on here?" Porras said, his voice drifting across the chasm. "You're supposed to be our inside man but you don't warn us about all this security. Jeez, anyone would think we were trying to snatch the President."

"The President's wife."

"What?"

"I just found out the President's wife is coming here tonight, man, that's why all the security—it's not for Otis."

"Well, that's just fucking great," Porras said.

His men were round the horseshoe curve and within about twenty yards of us.

"This ain't my fault," Perry said, "I did my part." He held out his hand. "Where's my fucking money? I want what's coming to me."

Porras looked at him for a moment. Put on a mock-Spanish accent.

"Sure thing, *gringo*." Then he shouted something in Spanish to the two men who were coming up the trail towards Bridget and me. They halted and turned back the way they had come.

*Get out of there*, I wanted to call. I was about to call. But Porras moved very quickly. He reached out, gripped Perry's left shoulder, turned him, and pushed.

I saw Perry's look of astonishment as he teetered for a moment then plunged headlong past the buttress down towards the river below. Porras raised his hand and gave a little farewell salute.

"Swim? The fall will probably kill you," I murmured.

Bridget, however, was more vocal. She stood up. I tried to pull her back down.

"You bastard!" she screamed, which puzzled me, since I didn't think she even liked Perry. "What have you done with my fucking Louis Vuitton suitcases?"

Ah. It took Porras a moment to locate the source of the shout. But then he looked across and peered through the undergrowth. When he saw us he grinned and called: "My journalist friends, how delightful to see you again."

I saw the two men nearest us raise their machine guns.

"Oh shit," I said.

"Oh shit," Bridget said.

"Oh shit," a bush beside us said, rising up with a machine gun held firmly in its, er, hands. A bush with a strong Cockney accent. Harry, our rescuer from the Amazon.

All around us other bushes rose up and were transformed into camouflaged men. Then all hell broke loose. Harry shot the two men who were nearest us on the trail. One of the bushes hustled Bridget and me back up the trail as the guerrillas and Harry's men exchanged deafening fire across the chasm.

I glanced back to see bullets splashing the rock face and the guerrillas falling like ninepins—they were totally exposed. But I couldn't see Porras. Was he already dead or had he slipped away again?

"He slipped away," Harry said to Ralph an hour later in the bar of the hotel in Aguas Calientes. Harry was still in his combat fatigues. He smelled faintly of cordite. "In the time it took me to pop the first two guerrillas Porras was up the trail and round the bend. I got a shot off but I don't know if I hit him.

"My men and some of the security forces are out looking for him but he knows this place better than we do. There's a thousand places to hole up."

"So he was after Otis—and Perry was feeding him information," Ralph said.

"Seems like it," Harry said. "I think he'd always planned that the kidnap happen here. He would have whisked Otis back down into the Amazonas—in a helicopter you can be there in a half hour. What threw him was all the extra security that's here because of the President's wife."

"Is he still around here someplace?" Ralph said. "Is he still a threat to the tour?"

"I think he's gone," Harry said. "Whatever his method was going to be his plan was dead the minute you put on the extra security. We killed or rounded up most of his men so he hasn't got the means to carry it out, even if he was foolhardy enough to try."

"But you'll carry on looking?" Ralph said.

"I'm locked on," Harry said. "I don't stop until I've got him—alive or dead."

"Jeez, this *is* like bloody Butch Cassidy," I said. I was having trouble coming to terms with what Harry had told us on the way back down here. "So the presidents of four countries, pissed off with the guerrillas for all the kidnappings and disruptions, are paying you and guys like you—"

"Elite units, yes."

"—to track down and kill a dozen of the leading drug barons and guerrilla leaders. In effect they've put bounties on these people's heads and you're modern-day bounty-hunters."

"Spot on."

"And you've been after Porras all the time?"

"He's our latest, yes. Slippery customer. We trailed him in the Amazon, lost him for a while but knew he'd end up here—we had wind of his plans."

"From who?"

He raised an eyebrow.

"Sources. But it looks like we saved your lives again."

I was remembering their cold-blooded killing of young Danilo.

"We had some trouble with the girl from the Amazon camp," I said.

"Oh?" Harry said, his smile still in place.

"She came looking for revenge on us because of what you did to her lover."

"Pretty little piece," he said. Shook his head. "There's fucking gratitude for you. We let her go. Strictly according to Hoyle we should have done her, too."

"But that's murder!" I said.

"Them's the rules," he said. "We get paid by the body."

"Jesus."

He looked at me levelly then got quickly to his feet.

"Pleased you're able to enjoy the rest of your life, Mr. Madrid." He nodded at Bridget. "Miss Frost."

He walked off, his shoes clacking on the tiled floor. I watched him through the window walk down the path towards the railway line. As he dropped from sight I was almost certain I saw a flash of color shift in the undergrowth. Someone in a red dress moving to follow.

I was looking morosely out of the window at the brown river below when I heard footsteps. I thought it was Bridget returning.

"You aren't too bright, you have no idea how to look after yourself in a tussle, but I gotta admit, Madrid, you have a god-damned astounding knack of being in the wrong place at the right time."

Ralph, big and solemn as ever, was looking at me. Richard stood beside him.

"Yeah, well, don't be thinking your troubles are over just because Harry and his Merry Men have wiped out most of Porras's guerrillas," I said.

"Meaning?"

"Meaning that either Mr. Otis Barnes, the Late Great, is as nutty as a fruitcake, has been sending himself death threats, and may have beaten Horace to death—"

"Say what?" Ralph said sharply, sitting forward in his chair. Richard walked to the window and looked out.

So I told them about my conversation with Otis about "Sinner Man" and about killing his parents. I told them about seeing him with Horace. Ralph listened intently. When I'd finished he steepled his hands in front of his face.

"You said 'either.' That means there's an 'or.'"

I sighed.

"Let me get back to you on the 'or.'"

Ralph dropped his hands.

"Okay, I've seen how Otis hates himself, I've seen my share of mental fuck-ups so, yeah, I can believe he's doing this for himself. That's how come the messages got into his room, his jacket pocket. But the question I have to ask is—what's he planning for Machu Picchu and is he a danger to anyone else when he's on stage?"

"Who knows?" I said. "But I don't think he's got an Uzi stashed in his guitar case if that's what you mean. What's your reason for the question?"

"The reason for the question," Richard said, turning from the window, "is that a phenomenal amount of time and money has been invested in tonight's concert and if there's any way at all it can go on, then it should."

"Even at the risk of people's lives?"

Richard thought for a moment.

"It should be possible, with all the security around, to stop Otis doing anything dangerous."

"Except maybe killing himself on prime-time TV."

"The show has to go on," Richard said grimly. "We don't know what Otis's mental state is."

I could see that from Richard's point of view all that mattered was the show. If it went up in flames he'd be one of those who got burned the most.

"We've got to speak to Conchita," Ralph said. "Find out about his mental state."

"What about Horace's death?" I said indignantly. "We can't just ignore it."

"You know, I don't figure that," Ralph said. "When I told Otis he seemed genuinely upset, even knowing the guy had been ripping him off."

"Yeah, well," I said. "I don't figure that either."

"Look Nick, Otis isn't going anywhere," Richard said. "He's hardly going to jump off the stage and do a runner is he? The cops are coming up tomorrow from Cusco to take statements from us anyway. They assume it was local villains."

I looked at him sharply.

"You're not suggesting we let Otis walk?"

"No, no—though I have to say in PR terms …"

"Stow that talk, mister," Ralph spoke quietly and firmly. "If Otis killed Horace he'll take the fall, I promise that."

Richard put his hands up in a calming gesture.

"Sure Ralph, I'm not saying otherwise. But what I am saying is that can wait until tomorrow."

"Which still leaves us with the problem of tonight," I said. "How do we ensure that Otis doesn't go bonkers on stage or that if he does he can be hustled off right quickly?"

Richard looked out of the window for a moment then gave me a speculative look. "I have a plan."

Half the Peruvian army was on maneuvers around the entrance to Machu Picchu when I reached there at six. Four helicopters were buzzing between the mountain peaks. The sun was already sinking low in the sky behind Huayc Picchu. The audience for the concert had been delivered in a convoy of buses up the zig zag road from Agua Calientes.

There were maybe 2,000 people settled on the terraces and as many again spread across the mountainside below the Gateway to the Sun. That was the notch in the mountain to the east of Machu Picchu, at the end of the Inca trail, through which you could see the sun rise each morning.

Raoul was overseeing security at the gate again.

"Everybody else here?" I said.

"Pretty much."

I headed along the walkway down past the audience, showed my pass, and went backstage.

The first ninety minutes of the concert passed in a blur. The support bands performed from various locations on the site, the light cannons fired off images at random across the performers, the audience, the mountain peaks around. The President's wife came and went. But I was too nervous to concentrate on any of it.

Not nervous about what Otis might do, although that concerned me. Nervous about what I was about to do.

Eventually it was time for Otis and his band to go on. I was standing at the side of the stage when he went by. He winked at me. He looked in good shape, bulking out his T-shirt as if he'd just finished a workout.

As Sukie and Venus walked by wearing very little they grinned, took my hands, and walked me on stage.

This was Richard's master plan. Otis wouldn't agree to have security guards onstage—thinking they were intended to protect him rather than be a protection from him. But Richard had persuaded him that for the sake of color in my article I should go on as one of the backing singers.

"Miming obviously," Richard insisted to me.

Well that was the plan. But when I got on stage behind the glare of the lights and I could hear the people on the terraces, glimpse wedges of them picked out at random by the light cannons, the two backing singers whooping and hollering, and the band tuning up and Otis doing a little dance—I must admit I lost it. I leaned into my microphone, raised both my arms above my head.

"Hello Peru!" I declaimed, in best rock star style.

I could hear bugger all of course—I didn"t have foldback, the speakers through which performers can monitor how they're doing. But I heard a swelling of applause and whistling from the audience beyond.

Otis seemed like his usual performing self, relaxed, dancing around, in great voice. I relaxed a little, too.

In fact once we got into the music I had a gas. I knew these songs and whilst a couple of times I doowopped when I should have doowahed I thought I did pretty well.

I was off some fifteen yards to the right of Otis. I could see little bits of business the two women were doing and I did my best to copy them. I dipped and shimmied and, you know, I think the audience responded to me.

I'd sung myself hoarse by the time Otis went into the slow closing section of his act. I could smell joss sticks on the still mountain air, thousands of them. I was pretty sweaty by then and breathless from singing. My lungs ached a bit from dragging the air in.

When Otis went into a plangent version of "Sinner Man" on solo guitar we backing singers had little to do but sway and click the odd finger. (I'd said no to a tambourine. Even I have my standards.)

Sukie and Venus had been looking my way, grinning and making comments to each other about my performance so I presumed I'd done pretty well. I wondered idly if I might be in with a chance with them. My breathlessness came on immediately.

I watched closely when Otis came to the lines: "And when you finally face yourself/Which of you comes out alive?" Did I imagine it or did he sing it with even more poignancy that usual? His eyes were closed, his head was tilted back—he was singing to the stars.

I wondered if he guessed that tomorrow he would have to answer for killing Horace.

The two lines were repeated twice more in the song. I could see Ralph off at the far side of the stage watching intently. I nodded to him as I swayed, then he turned away to talk to one of the guards.

On the second repetition of the lines I was aware of

movement to my right. I looked and stood stock still as a man walked on stage.

It was Otis Barnes.

I'd half expected this but even so I was rooted to the spot. This was my "or" from my earlier "either ... or" formulation. Open-mouthed I watched as he walked past me towards the Otis Barnes who had been singing all evening. I took in the clothes—the same black jeans and T-shirt, Otis's uniform. He was taller than the other Otis, not as bulky.

Otis—the real one, I was presuming—glanced to his side. He saw the thing he'd always feared. Himself.

He stopped, the line frozen on his lips, his fingers frozen on the strings of his guitar. His *doppelganger* walked right up to him.

I was rooted to the spot. I looked imploringly over at Ralph. He was looking back on stage but from his angle could only see one Otis. He looked perplexed that the singing had stopped.

Everything happened at once. As the doppelganger reached Otis, I finally stirred, grabbing my microphone stand and starting towards them. But before I could reach them, the doppelganger raised the pistol in his right hand and shot Otis twice in the chest.

# SIXTEEN

Otis fell back. His double took two steps to the end of the stage and dropped off it into the darkness below just as I swung at him with the mike stand.

Missing him, I overbalanced, the microphone whacked the stage and bounced back and the lead whipped round my legs. I sprawled full length, tensed for some kind of electric shock. Nothing happened.

I looked up. Ralph was kneeling beside Otis. As I heard Sukie and Venus start to scream and a delayed gasp from the audience, I couldn't help but notice that the microphone lead that snaked round my legs was not plugged into the amplifiers.

The bastards. I'd given the performance of a lifetime and nobody had heard a bloody thing. I'd spent all night singing into a dead mike. Snarling, I jumped off the stage and set off in pursuit of Otis's double.

I saw him lumbering towards Huayc Picchu. The high peak was bathed in light, the weird symbols drifting across it. I hurried through the deserted ruins—this part of Machu Picchu wasn't being used for the concert. My quarry was about fifty yards ahead. He wasn't hurrying but he was moving steadily. For a moment he was silhouetted in a sharp beam of light and I saw him toss the gun away.

I wondered if it was the gun he'd taken from the man he'd beaten half to death outside the nightclub in Bogota. I had no doubt he had done that, not Otis. He had probably killed Horace, too—I recalled the puzzled look on the manager's face as he was led into the alley. Puzzled because he suspected the Otis he was with wasn't the Otis he knew.

As I followed, I rejigged the events of the past few days. This was the man who'd told me about murdering his parents. Who better to deliver death threats to Otis's bedroom and dressing room than someone everyone mistook for Otis? Even following us to Baza to spray-paint the Mercedes wouldn't have been difficult.

Ralph had said something in Lima about Otis losing his backstage pass and needing another one. I guessed that was the double getting access. And once he had a pass he could come and go as he pleased. That explained why Otis had not been where he was supposed to be on Machu Picchu earlier in the day. It was the double Raoul had let through first. And once on the site, he'd gone to ground until he deemed the time was right.

I wondered how long he'd been stalking Otis. Maybe his existence explained other things in Otis's life that Otis had no memory of. But two questions remained—who was this guy and what did he have in mind? When the doppelganger replaces its original, what happens then?

Okay, three questions.

As chases go it wasn't the most exciting you'd ever see. Once we reached the base of Huayc Picchu we only went 300 yards—though it did take forty-five minutes. The steepness of the trail and the bloody altitude again.

He saw me as the track dipped before striking up the almost sheer side of the peak. He set off at a run up the slope.

Within ten yards he needed to stop to catch his breath. I got to within an arm's length of him when I had to make my stop.

At which point, glancing back over his shoulder so I could see his red face and open, gasping mouth, he started off again.

He slowed to a walk after five yards and ground to a halt again after a further ten. Bent over clutching his knees, I could hear him sucking in air but I wasn't in any position to do anything about it. I was standing head back, hands on hips, dragging in great lungfuls of non-existent air. My heart was beating like a triphammer.

And so it went on—stop start, stop start. It reminded me of some elegant mathematical theory I'd read once proving that logically you can never get from A to B. You get halfway then you go half the subsequent distance, then half of then half again …

That was pretty much how I was feeling after fifteen minutes, by which time we were both reduced to shuffling a few yards then stopping to look at the view.

Except for the heavy panting we made no sounds. He would look down at me, his face red but expressionless. I thought of shouting something to him but I didn't have the breath to spare.

My legs were dead weights but I forced myself to keep moving. The heaviness in my limbs was getting worse, my throat and chest were aching from the exertion just from the effort to breathe.

The path began to zigzag. By now we were moving in and out of darkness as the light-shapes floated across the side of the mountain. I thought I would zig instead of zag and gained a couple of yards by scrambling up the slope between the two lengths of path.

I was now no more than six yards behind him and could smell his sweat as he forced himself on.

I caught him up when he was partway up a short flight of steps the Incas had cut out of the rock face 500 years before. He lost his footing on the third step and slid back. I grabbed him by his belt and wrenched him down.

With hindsight it was the wrong thing to do. He fell on top of me, knocking what little air I had left out of my lungs. It took only a moment to realize I had no strength for a fight. The knowledge that he wouldn't have either was little comfort since he was sprawled across me like a beached whale. If I couldn't get him off his body-weight would flatten me like a cartoon cat.

He was remarkably inert. I tried heaving. Nothing. I tried wriggling. Not a thing. Finally, with an immense effort, I rolled him off me and got up on all fours, gasping for air. Strange shapes floated before my eyes. I felt horribly dizzy.

He was crouched, one hand on the floor in front of him, glaring at me balefully. He was summoning the energy to jump me. I staggered to my feet. As he lunged I swung a punch that was farcical in its lack of power.

My fist glanced off his jaw, not slowing him in the least. He wrapped his arms around me and tried a head-butt. The effort was too much for both of us and we fell over again. There was no strength in his embrace. I struggled free and got to my feet again.

This was humiliating. I looked around and saw a stone about twice the size of my hand. I picked it up and as he was getting to his feet hit him on the back of his head. He went down.

I searched him. He had his passport in his back pocket. The name in it was Otis Barnes. Puzzled, I checked the date of birth. It was the same as Otis's. I was contemplating a *Man In the Iron Mask* scenario until I twigged. This was Otis's passport—he'd stolen it from Otis's room. I was willing to bet Otis was carrying this man's without realizing it.

"I know imitation is the sincerest form of flattery," I said. "But what's going on here? Why this fixation with Otis?"

He was propped against a rock, blood dribbling down the side of his face. I was standing off to one side, the stone still in my hand.

"Because he's me and I'm him," he mumbled. "He knows—that's why he wrote 'Sinner Man.' He's been following me around, you know."

"Sure, sure. Look, you've got to help me with this because I don't understand. Is it chance that you look so much like him? Or are you actually related?"

"He stole my fucking life!" he said. "I used to see him on the folk circuit. We both gigged. It could have been either one of us. Either one. But he got the breaks." He lapsed into silence.

Looking at him I could see that the resemblance was nowhere near perfect. The doppelganger was taller but less muscular than Otis. The facial resemblance was achieved more by extras—beard, hair, glasses.

It had clearly helped the imposter to know that Otis wore the same clothes combination as a kind of uniform wherever he was. Black 501s, black T-shirt, and shades. Of course that meant he could have been the doppelganger for 80 percent of the people in music, the media, and advertising …

I remembered some of the horrific things he'd told me about his childhood. Maybe that explained it. Then again, maybe it didn't.

"But why did you shoot him? Surely that's like killing yourself?"

He looked up at me with hard eyes, the blood still dribbling down the side of his head.

"I didn't kill Otis. I killed an imposter. I'm him—surely you understand that?"

"You're a bit too post-modern for me," I said, just as the first security guard reached us.

Ralph and the others had all gone down to the hotel when I got back to the stage. I couldn't find out from anyone if Otis was alive or dead. Crowds were still milling around outside the gate but the double was hurried through to a jeep with a blanket over his head and driven down the mountain.

I was dropped off at the gate to the hotel in another jeep. I went over to Bridget's bungalow. Her door was ajar but there was no sign of her. I walked outside and looked down the path towards the river. The path was lit by soft lights concealed in the undergrowth. Bridget was walking alongside Ferdinand Porras.

I called after them. Although the noise the river made was tremendous they both heard my hoarse cry. They turned.

Porras had a gun pressed to Bridget's side. She was clutching her handbag, one hand inside it.

Porras looked at me and shouted something. In the roar of the river behind him I couldn't make it out. He gestured with the gun. Bridget didn't move. He grabbed her arm angrily. She swung round, bringing her hand out of the handbag, and whacked him in the face. He swayed and the gun dropped from his hand.

Bridget fell back with a horrified expression on her face. I could see something sticking out of Porras's left eye, blood gouting out around it. I heard an animal bellow of pain above the unremitting roar of the river as he stumbled like a wounded beast and put his hand to the thing that was stuck in his eye socket.

I ran close as he tottered on the very edge of the path, flailing wildly with one arm, one eye wide and fixed on Bridget. I could hear his bellow of pain and rage more clearly as I closed the gap between us. Blood was pouring down his face, soaking his shirt and trousers.

He reached up and plucked the thing from his eye. He looked at it with his one good eye, then at Bridget. Something between exasperation and resignation passed over his features as he let the object drop to the floor. His knees buckled and he fell backwards. I reached Bridget in time to see Porras hit the water. He was immediately tugged into the flow. His body bounced from rock to rock and was carried away on the surge of the water. Heading yet again for the Amazon.

Bridget was shaking. I put my arms round her so we could shake together. We both looked down at the teak dolphin I'd bought an age ago on the Amazon, it's thin, curved tail dripping with blood.

I don't know how long we stood there hugging each other but when we turned to go back to our bungalows, Otis's doppelganger was blocking our way.

"Shit, not again," I said, then looked more closely.

"Otis?" I said, leading Bridget down the path towards the figure.

"Damned right," he growled. He was wearing the same T-shirt as before. Where were the bullet holes, where were the bandages?

"But how?" I said. "He shot you twice."

Otis fingered the T-shirt.

"Haven't you heard? They can bullet-proof anything these days."

# EPILOGUE

Bridget and I were sitting at a table at the rear of the Bogota Magic Circle's club. Ernest Beacon had already debriefed us. The doppelganger was locked away in a Peruvian prison cell. I didn't rate his chances of survival.

I'd asked casually about Harry, the bounty hunter, but Ernest hadn't heard from him. Nothing strange in that. Necessarily.

Now he joined us again, seating himself rather gingerly. He had the worst-fitting dinner jacket I'd ever seen. It was far too big for him.

"Bomb-proof?"

He shook his head.

"My performance jacket."

When he sat down he carefully patted his pockets then gingerly put his hand inside his jacket.

I assumed he was looking for cigarettes but his hand came out empty. He wriggled a little.

"I'm up next," he whispered. "My debut. Just waiting for them to call my name."

A voice reverberated from the speaker above our heads.

"And now will you please welcome Ernie Beacon."

"Ernest at work, Ernie here," he said as he waddled down the aisle and took the steps to the stage two at a time. I realized now why the dinner jacket was so big.

"What was all that wriggling about?" Bridget said.

"Trying not to squash his pigeons," I said. "His pockets are full of them."

"Naturally. I thought they used rubber ones, otherwise they'd have a pocket full of pigeon shit after a week of regular bookings."

Ernie produced two pigeons in quick succession. He didn't get the action quite right with either of them. The first time he proffered it nervously, as if afraid it was going to peck him after being cooped up in his jacket pocket. He seemed frankly surprised the second one was still alive.

I'd been worried about Bridget. Injuring Porras in such a brutal way was a terrible thing for anyone to cope with. But she'd gone back to her usual self the previous day when we'd said our goodbyes to Otis and Richard. I'd also been worried what effect meeting his doppelganger would have on Otis, but he too had seemed jubilant.

"Well, it's the perfect get-out, isn't it?" Richard said. "If Conchita catches him out he can say, wasn't me, must have been someone impersonating me."

"She won't fall for that," I said.

"I suggested he had his johnson bullet-proofed just in case—though I don't know how the stuff works with knives."

It was when Richard invited us to dinner that I realized Bridget was on the mend.

"Got the chief of some remote Amazonian tribe coming to dinner with us—thought you might like to sit next to him, Bridget."

"Forget it—I don't talk to yokels."

"Yokels? This guy's from a Stone Age tribe whose ways are unchanged for 2,000 years, for God's sake."

"If his ways have been unchanged for 2,000 years we're not

going to have much to talk about are we? Maybe berries or a hundred things to do with wood lice. And your starter for ten is rubbery plants."

Richard ploughed on. "He can trace his lineage back to the last chief of the Incas."

"And what's so special about the Incas? According to my friend Professor Madrid here, the entire Inca nation was defeated by a dozen Spaniards because the Incas were frightened of one horse. Like I said—yokels.

"It's that double standard you see," she carried on, in full flow now, "what's the difference between a boring person in the English countryside and here—nothing except the plate through the lip, and not everybody in Sussex wears those."

"You're very chipper," I said to Richard, "considering the concert ended in disaster."

I was angry with him since I'd discovered that not only hadn't they miked me up, they also hadn't lit me for the film. I'd been totally in the dark throughout the entire show—no cheap comments, please—except when I fell over on stage with the microphone, and they explained that away by saying I was a drunk who'd broken through security.

"What do you mean?" Richard said now.

"I mean Geoff Bartram walking out and shooting the star of the show, what do you think I mean?"

I'd been right about the passports—Otis was carrying one for a Geoff Bartram.

Richard laughed.

"The audience thought that was part of the show. Fitting climax to the song to have the doppelganger appear. They went nuts."

Back in the club Bridget nudged me.

"Did you notice Otis was still off with me this morning?" she said as Ernest left the stage to mild applause. "And after all I did for him. You'd think we'd never spent the night together."

I should have changed the subject but I couldn't think of anything to say. I'd been dreading this moment ever since I'd given some thought to what Geoff Bartram had been up to whilst masquerading as Otis.

The silence hung between us. Then Bridget began to wail.

# AUTHOR'S NOTE

In researching *Two to Tango* I found the following books useful: *Simon Strong: Whitewash, Pablo Escobar, and the Cocaine Wars* (Pan 1996); *The South American Handbook*, 72nd edition (Trade & Travel Handbooks 1996); *Peter Frost: Exploring Cusco* (Nuevas Imagenes 1989).

Just as I completed this novel my knowledge of the hostage-taking situation in Colombia was enhanced by a magazine article: "Adventures in the Ransom Trade" by William Prochnau *(Vanity Fair* May 1998).

# *No Laughing Matter*

## by Peter Guttridge

Tom Sharpe meets Raymond Chandler in *No Laughing Matter* a humorous and brilliant debut that will keep readers on a knife's edge of suspense until the bittersweet end.

When a naked woman flashes past Nick Madrid's hotel window, it's quite a surprise. For Madrid's room is on the fourteenth floor, and the hotel doesn't have an outside elevator. The management is horrified when Cissie Parker lands in the swimming pool—not only is she killed, but she makes a real mess of the shallow end.

In Montreal for the Just for Laughs festival, Madrid, a journalist who prefers practicing yoga to interviewing the stars, turns gumshoe to answer the question: Did she fall or was she pushed? The trail leads first to the mean streets of Edinburgh and then to Los Angeles, where the truth lurks among the dark secrets of Hollywood.

" ... a near laugh-riot."

—*Library Journal*

0-9725776-4-5

speck

# *A Ghost of a Chance*
## by Peter Guttridge

Nick Madrid isn't exactly thrilled when his best friend in journalism—OK, his *only* friend in journalism—the "Bitch of the Broadsheets," Bridget Frost, commissions him to spend a night in a haunted place on the Sussex Downs and live to tell the tale. Especially as living to tell the tale isn't made an urgent priority.

But Nick stumbles on a hotter story when he discovers a dead man hanging upside down from an ancient oak. Why was he killed? Is there a connection to the nearby New Age conference center? Or to *The Great Beast*, the Hollywood movie about Aleister Crowley, filming down in Brighton?

New Age meets the Old Religion as Nick is bothered, bewildered, but not necessarily bewitched by pagans, satanists, and a host of assorted metaphysicians. Séances, sabbats, a horse-ride from hell, and a kick-boxing zebra all come Nick's way as he obstinately tracks a treasure once in the possession of Crowley.

0-9725776-8-8

speck

# DeKok and the Geese of Death

## by Baantjer

"Baantjer has created an odd police detective who roams Amsterdam interacting with the widest possible range of antisocial types.
This series is the answer to an insomniac's worst fears."

—*The Boston Globe*

Baantjer brings to life Inspector DeKok in another stirring pot-
boiler full of suspenseful twists and unusual conclusions.

In *The Geese of Death*, DeKok takes on Igor Stablinsky, a man accused
of bludgeoning a wealthy old man and his wife. To DeKok's unfailing
eye the killing urge is visibly present in the suspect during questioning, but did he commit this particular crime?

All signs point to one of the few remaining estates in Holland.
The answer lies within a strange family, suspicions of incest, deadly
geese, and a horrifying mansion. Baantjer's perceptive style brings
to light the essences of his characters, touching his audience with
subtle wit and irony.

0-9725776-6-1

speck

# *Bullets*

## by Steve Brewer

When a contract killer bumps off a high roller in a Las Vegas casino, a tangle of romance, gambling, and gunplay follows. The killer, Lily Marsden, is a mysterious and cold woman who is a true professional. But soon, the casino owner, his henchmen, and the victim's two brothers are on Lily's trail.

Former Chicago cop Joe Riley is pursuing Lily, too. She cost him his job as a homicide investigator when suspicion of a bookie's murder fell on him. Joe is certain Lily killed the bookie, and he's tracked her across the country to Vegas.

Throw in some local cops, a playboy, a new widow, a rug merchant, a harridan, and a couple of idiot gamblers named Delbert and Mookie, and the mixture soon boils with intrigue and murder. Add a dash of romance as a strange magnetism develops between Lily and Joe, dust the whole concoction with Steve Brewer's trademark humor, and you end up with *Bullets*—a crime novel you won't soon forget.

0-9725776-7-X

For a complete catalog of *speck press* books please contact us at
the following:

speck press
po box 102004
denver, co 80250, usa
e: books@speckpress.com
t: 800-996-9783
f: 303-756-8011
w: speckpress.com


All of our books are available through your local bookseller.